THE SOLITARY

THE SOLITARY

LYNN HALL

COLLIER BOOKS
Macmillan Publishing Company   New York

Copyright © 1986 by Lynn Hall
All rights reserved. No part of this book may be reproduced or transmitted in any form or by any means, electronic or mechanical, including photocopying, recording, or by any information storage and retrieval system, without permission in writing from the Publisher.
Collier Books
Macmillan Publishing Company
866 Third Avenue, New York, NY 10022
Collier Macmillan Canada, Inc.
First Collier Books edition 1989
Printed in the United States of America
A hardcover edition of *The Solitary* is available from Charles Scribners Sons, Macmillan Publishing Company.

10 9 8 7 6 5 4 3 2 1

Library of Congress Cataloging-in-Publication Data
Hall, Lynn.
The solitary/Lynn Hall. — 1st Collier Books ed.   p.   cm.
Summary: With her mother in prison for killing her father, seventeen-year-old Jane seeks to escape her past and find self-reliance breeding rabbits on their Arkansas homestead.
ISBN 0-02-043315-8
[1. Self-reliance — Fiction. 2. Rabbit breeding — Fiction 3. Family problems — Fiction. 4. Arkansas — Fiction.] I. Title.
PZ7.H1458Sn 1989 [Fic] — dc19   89-7359   CIP   AC

THE SOLITARY

ONE

Highway 295 is a narrow blacktop road as faded and patched as old jeans. It loops in no special hurry through the wooded hills of northwest Arkansas, past retirement acreages with pastel bungalows, over rusted iron bridges. Along its edges the blacktop crumbles and gives way to powerful weeds pushing up through its crust.

On a January afternoon a few years ago, a dent-dimpled blue Ford pickup pulled off of 295 four miles south of Prosper and rolled to a stop. A wiry man in jeans and sheepskin jacket got out and began lifting cartons and grocery bags down from the back of the truck and stacking them by the roadside. Two women climbed out on the passenger side, jammed their fists into jacket pockets, and watched the unloading.

One woman was small and slim and wore a sheepskin jacket like her husband's. The other figure was taller, straighter, younger. She stood at a little distance, already pulling away.

1

Jane Cahill was long and lean, both in figure and features, with prominent overlapping teeth and not enough chin to balance the profile. Her skin was coarse textured, her brows shaggy and straight. From the shadow of the brows, clear blue-gray eyes looked out with a steadfast hopelessness, as though the prisoner behind the unfortunate face had despaired of rescue.

Her hair was a kinky flair of brown around her face. The hood of her jacket lay back at half-mast, exposing red-rimmed ears. Her sharp nose was reddened, too, and lung-shaped clouds of breath floated from her lips. She watched the unloading process wordlessly. She seldom spoke; when she did, her voice, like her face, was textured with character.

Jane looked from the pile of her belongings to the rocky track that led almost invisibly back into the woods behind her but said nothing. She didn't argue with Doyle. She never had.

The man finished the unloading and stood facing Jane. Belligerently he said, "I told you I'd never set foot on that place again, and I meant it. Besides, that road ain't been used in twelve years. If it ain't washed out, the rocks would chew up my tires. I told you I'd bring you this far, and I done it. Now we'll stop at the closest neighbor and see if somebody'll haul your things in for you. That's the best I can do."

The woman in the matching jacket said, "Janey, you don't have to do this. Wait till spring, anyway. You don't even know if the house is still standing, much less if there's any way to get heat in it. You come on back home now and let this business wait till spring."

Jane shook her head. Now that the moment was here, she wanted only for them to be gone. She'd waited twelve years to be free of them. Within her lanky frame burned a need for aloneness so strong it overrode her qualms about surviving here on her own and her fears of the house that waited for her at the end of the rock road.

Her uncle moved around the truck and got into it, evading her gaze. "Come on, Marlyce. We got a long drive home. If this is what she wants, leave her to it. She's as crazy as her mother. . . ." His voice disappeared down his jacket front and was lost under engine noise.

Marlyce darted forward and gave Jane a swift, awkward hug. They hadn't been a hugging family. "You just get to a phone and call me if you need anything, or if you want to change your mind and move home again, hear?"

In spite of her intense relief when the truck pulled away, Jane felt a pull of sadness, too. Marlyce had been decent to her within the limits of her husband's approval, and twelve years was two-thirds of Jane's life. That old life was over now and a new one beginning. "Be careful what you wish for, you might get it," she told herself wryly.

Squatting beside the grocery bags, she sorted through her belongings and rearranged them till she had two bags of necessities, food and night things, and her purse with the money in it. The rest she left beside the road with the hope that Doyle would actually find someone to haul them in for her before they were snowed on or stolen.

With a bag in each arm and her denim shoulder purse banging off her hip, she began the trek home. The new sheepskin-lined boots felt good between her feet and the snow-frosted rocks; she was glad she'd spent the money for them.

3

An inch or two of snow covered the woods floor in a lacy pattern, showing greens and browns in sheltered patches under leaves and sticks. Some of the oak trees still held last year's russet leaves along with the snow that etched their branches. Squirrels and blue jays followed her, scolding at her intrusion into their territory.

The road was a double path of red rocks, grown through with weeds. It led up and down small hills, across a streambed that was dry now but would wash out in the spring. In places the road had disintegrated into small gulleys that would indeed have stopped Doyle's truck. Looking at them, Jane wondered if she would have to carry her things back in, one box at a time, after all.

"Maybe I *am* as crazy as my mother."

But she'd never believed her mother was crazy at all, even though the rest of her world thought so. Jane believed her mother had been infinitely courageous. Of course that might mean that she herself was crazy along with her mother. It was a possibility she'd lived with all her growing-up years.

Her arms began to ache from their hold on the shopping bags; her legs ached from the unaccustomed walk over the rough and hilly track. In spite of her height, Jane Cahill was no athlete. She'd never played basketball in school, or softball or volleyball except in gym classes when there was no escape from it.

By nature she was not a team player. They hadn't wanted her on their teams and she hadn't wanted them, those normal, average popular girls. They'd never quite forgotten that she was the daughter of Evangeline Cahill;

they'd steered around her and stared through her and shot knowing looks at one another in the periphery of her vision, and they'd gone along with their own mothers' gentle suggestions that they find someone else to play with.

Gradually Jane had quit creeping off to cry in corners and hiding in the rest room at recess. As she grew older, she developed control over her expression and her tears and held within her both the pain and the belief that she had earned it and deserved it.

She'd made herself too busy to care. At ten she found lawn-mowing customers; at twelve she was baby-sitting regularly. Last summer, at sixteen, she'd worked for an auto parts shop, delivering repair parts to service stations around Rogers. The money she earned was more important than having friends or being on teams: it was vital to her goal.

Part of her earnings had gone to Aunt Marlyce for her food, part had gone for school clothes and expenses. For the past four years she'd been fiercely independent of Doyle Cahill's money. He might hate her, but he couldn't say she was costing him anything.

The rest of her earnings had gone into the fund, which bopped against her hip now with every step. Six hundred thirty-four dollars and change. On that she would have to survive somehow, permanently. No power on earth would make her go back to Doyle Cahill's house in Rogers. Starving to death would be better. At least starving could be done alone.

Just as she was seriously wondering if Doyle had let her out at the wrong road, Jane saw sunlight ahead. The clearing. Her own place, where nobody else had a right to be. . . . The solitude she ached for lay just ahead, solitude and shelter from people with unkind eyes.

At the edge of the clearing she stopped to take it in. The house was still standing, and the barn behind it. Foot-high grass, sparse and weedy, lay unmarked between her and the house. No one had been here for a long, long time.

The house was much smaller than she remembered. Its gray boards showed no sign of paint. The porch that spanned the front side of the rectangular building was rotten and sagging, and part of its roof was gone. Many of the small windowpanes were broken or missing. Still, it was better than she'd feared. The place might have burned down or rotted away in those twelve years.

With the impact of a body blow the memory came back. The loud explosion of her father's squirrel gun had blasted her out of her sleep. She sat up in her loft bed, startled, a scrawny five-year-old child with bird's-nest hair and a face that was never completely clean. She sat there, heart pounding, a terrible fear already filling her, as though she knew instinctively what had happened. She stayed frozen in position in her bed, needing to get up and use the potty under the bed but afraid.

Then her mother's face appeared at floor level, above the loft ladder. "Get up and get dressed, Janey. Wear your good dress. We're going to town."

"With Pa?"

"No. Not with Pa."

Her mother spoke not another word while Jane dressed and used the potty and descended the loft ladder, nor while

Evangeline pulled shut the door to the parental bedroom, looked for a long, blank moment at the squirrel gun on the sofa, then ushered Janey outdoors and into the jeep.

She didn't speak during the two-hour drive north to Rogers, to Pine Street, to Uncle Doyle's house. In the driveway Evangeline turned at last and said, "Go inside. They'll take care of you. I'm sorry I couldn't shoot myself, too, and make it easier for you. I want you to forget about me now. Go on. Go!" At the end she'd screamed at the child, who needed the scream to get her out of the jeep and up the walk to Uncle Doyle's front door.

Only later, gradually, did Janey begin to understand that her mother was not coming back. Her mother was in the state women's reformatory, serving twenty years for shooting her husband through the chest with his own squirrel gun as he lay sleeping in his bed, in this house in this clearing.

With courage akin to her mother's, Jane Cahill crossed the clearing and approached the house.

TWO

Jane's senses overwhelmed her with memory as she stood just inside the door. Beneath the smells of dust and rot, mouse droppings and mildew, was the subtle scent of her childhood. The dark reds and blues of the linoleum underfoot, worn in patterns of the planks beneath it, held memories of games played on that floor while her mother cooked dinner.

Jacks. She'd had a game of jacks given to her at Christmas, a small rubber ball and spikey handful of metal jacks. She'd tried and tried to get past threesies, but her five-year-old fist was too small and too slow.

Then Pa had stepped on a jack in his bare feet and grabbed Janey and shaken her until her neck nearly snapped, his face huge and dark and animal-like. He'd thrown her against the wall. . . .

Jane shook her head. "This is my place now," she said aloud in her strong sandpaper voice.

She stepped on in and set the bags down on a wobble-legged pine table in the center of the room. Beyond was the black hulk of the wood stove and a crude kitchen counter with open shelves above it. A back door opened on to a grassy area behind the house and overgrown paths to woodpile and outhouse. On the wall to the right was a sagging purple sofa, the ladder to the loft room above, and the door to the bedroom, the house's only other room.

"Get it over with," she said aloud. Her own voice, even talking to herself, sounded better to her than the utter stillness of the house. She moved to the bedroom door and opened it. Beyond was the iron bedstead, stripped to the blue-and-white-striped mattress that still showed a plate-sized brown stain, her father's blood. Rag rug on the floor, two peeling veneer chairs, one straight and one rocker, a dresser similarly peeling. In the end wall was a stone fireplace, which was the little house's one claim to quality. It was small and built of local stone, and it had never been used in Jane's memory, but it was a fireplace.

Her eyes were pulled back to the brown stain on the mattress. Again she heard the dreadful blast of the gun, but now she could see, with sickening clarity, her father lying faceup, a startled expression frozen onto his features by death. He wore a gray one-piece suit of long underwear, and in the middle of his chest a stain of red was slowly spreading. His fingers were outstretched, as though reaching for the throat of his wife. . . .

White-faced and clammy, Jane backed out of the room. The vision was too clear for imagination. A ghost, then? Some sort of imprint of tragedy left in the room?

9

Will I have to live with that? she wondered with despair. *Is he going to drive me out of here? I can't let him. This is my place in the world now, and I'm not going to let him spoil it for me.*

Clenching her jaw she opened the bedroom door again. There was nothing on the bed now except the bloodstain, although the atmosphere of the room seemed charged with echoes of tragedy. "All in my head," she said grimly and gripped the corner of the mattress. By hauling and twisting at it she overturned it to expose a more brightly striped side, marked only by crisscross lines of rust from the metal springs below.

"If there's anyone living in there, you can just get out now," she warned, pounding the mattress. No mice appeared, although one corner had been chewed and the cotton stuffing pulled free. She hit it a few more whacks and raised three spiders, which she mashed.

"I will sleep in this bed, in this room, tonight and every other night of my life," she said more loudly than was necessary. It was a pact with herself as well as a warning to her father.

Back in the kitchen, she stood trying to think what to do first. There was so much. Everything needed to be done all at once, and yet she couldn't find a starting point. She felt drifty, detached. For the first time in her memory she was independent of time. Seven o'clock, get up. Eight-thirty, be in her seat in her first class. Eleven-forty to twelve-ten, lunch period. Saturday, up early to get her part of the housecleaning done so she could go to her Saturday job. Sunday, go to Sunday School and church to placate Uncle

10

Doyle, who went on year after year looking at her as though she contained the devil that had killed his brother. The bits of time that weren't demanded of her by others, Jane used to pull herself into herself in whatever solitude she could find, at the park or the library or wherever, to live in her dreams for escape.

She stood leaning her hips against the wooden table and looking around her, feeling waves of tentative joy rippling over her, dispelling the trembling aftermath of her confrontation in the bedroom. The bad part of her life was over now; she felt that as strongly as she'd ever felt anything.

She went to the door and opened it and stood looking across the clearing at the woods that sheltered her from the world.

"Yay . . . hoo!" It was a joyful shout.

Leaving the house, she jumped the hole in the porch and ran across the clearing, bounding like a child. The land sloped gently downhill, then dropped a few feet into a creek bed in which clear water and the rocky bottom could be seen through a skin of ice. Looking upstream, Jane could just see the spring, a few yards into the woods. The creek curved there, turning against an outcropping of rock and disappearing from sight. An iron pipe had been driven into the face of the rock and tapped into an underground spring, so that even in January, water flowed from the pipe and down into the creek. Just below the rope of water was the food safe, an animal-tight metal box set lid-deep in the icy water to refrigerate food.

Between Jane and the spring, uphill to her left, stood the barn. So much depended on what was left inside it. She left the creek and climbed toward it, chanting hopes under her breath.

The barn was long and low, roofed in rusted metal, sided with oak planks more substantial than those in the house's walls. Holding her breath to freeze her hope, Jane forced back the solidly rusted door handle and pulled.

The barn was dim inside but cleaner smelling than the house had been. Something scurried away in the far end, but she didn't see what it was. Her eyes were on the important part—the cages. They were still there in a long row against the back wall, stretching the full sixty feet of the barn's length.

She let out her breath in a long sigh and moved forward for a closer look. The wire mesh of the cages was crusted with ancient filth. The crockery water dishes were full of dust and dead flies; many were cracked. Wisps of twelve-year-old hay still lay in some of the cages. But it was there, the precious equipment! It was all workable, cleanable, possible. She emerged into the winter sunlight with a smile of triumph illuminating her face.

The sun was lower now, and cooler. "The stove," she said. "Wood. Heat."

Beside the back door she found a small stack of firewood, broken branches and a few split lengths, and a helter-skelter pile of big chunks of tree trunks, aged gray and dry. So much for that problem. Optimistically she went inside for a look at the stove.

The hundreds of hours she'd spent in the Rogers Public Library had not all been spent in idle escapism. From the time, two years ago, when her plan had begun taking solid shape, Jane had used those hours to read, almost to memorize, everything she could find that would help her. First the rabbit books, then gardening, heating with wood and cooking on wood stoves, preserving, even hunting and fishing and trapping magazines, although she shuddered away from anything requiring killing.

The important thing about wood stoves, she remembered, was to be sure the stovepipes were cleaned out and safely distant from burnable surfaces and not rusted through anywhere. She stood a long time before her stove, studying it—massive, black cast iron squatting on a tin floor-protector. Silver-handled doors in the front opened on to firebox and oven. The top of the stove was flat, with round cut-out lids, which could be lifted by prying them up with a wire-spring-handled tool. With the lids removed, the holes became burners over the fire within. Along one side of the firebox was a large pouchlike water reservoir, to hold a constant supply of heated water.

From the back of the stove the chimney pipe rose and would have jogged back and up into a brick chimney but for a length of pipe that was missing. The remaining sections, from what Jane could see, were packed full of something, nests or soot or rags. The oven door hung loose, a broken hinge dangling.

"That's just impossible," she muttered. "Well then, that leaves the fireplace." Back in the bedroom, she ignored the bed, knelt, and stuck her head inside the fireplace and twisted to look up the chimney. It, too, was cluttered with dark bulges, but some sky glimmered at the end. Hope.

In the barn she looked for a pole of some kind, long

enough to reach the length of the chimney, but couldn't find one and settled instead for a piece of heavy, rusted chain. With the chain over one shoulder she clawed her way up onto the porch roof by standing on a wobbly piece of railing at one end of the porch.

Uncomfortably aware of the rotted boards beneath her hands and knees, she crawled up onto the house roof and on up until she straddled the ridge. Looking down at the ground made her dizzy, so she focused on the rock chimney at the end of the roof instead and began inching her way toward it.

If I fall off this thing, nobody's going to find me and get me to a hospital. Maybe I should get down and find somebody to do it for me. No. I can't afford to hire people for things like this. I wanted to take care of myself, so I'd better start doing it. Okay. I will.

The rounded red-and-tan rocks of the chimney were a welcome anchor when she reached them. She found that the metal cap over the chimney hole came off, with a little forcing. She set it between her leg and the chimney and began feeding the chain down, down, down.

Awkwardly at first and then with gathering enthusiasm she swung the chain in circles and listened to the song of it clanking against the metal chimney liner. Stuff rained down inside, and clouds of black creosote rose toward her face, making her pull away and grimace against the acrid black stuff.

Finally she looked down the chimney and saw that it was a cleared tube all the way to the floor of the fireplace.

"I did it," she yelled. "I'll get a fire started so the

14

house will be warming up. Then I better go back out to the road and start hauling in some more stuff. Blankets. Something to cook in and eat off." She dreaded the thought of carrying all those boxes and bags over the hilly rocky miles.

Cautiously she began inching backward toward the porch roof. She was about to turn and slide down toward it when she heard a car engine in the distance, growing louder. In a few seconds a green Bronco bounced into the clearing and came to a stop beneath her. A man got out and stood looking around.

"Up here," Jane called. He looked up, startled. He was middle-aged and roundly pleasant looking, with bald head and a startlingly black full beard. He shaded his eyes and squinted up at her.

"I was told there was a damsel in distress back here, and what do I find but a chimney sweep. Here, let me help you down from there."

He couldn't reach her to help, but his upstretched arms steadied Jane by their presence and she landed intact. She peered around him and saw her bags and boxes in the rear of the Bronco. A rare, full-blown smile beautified her face.

"You brought my things. Thank you. I was afraid I was going to have to carry it all in on foot. Are you my neighbor?"

"First place south of here on the highway. Beau Smith, by name. You're..."

"Jane. Cahill." She tensed, waiting for his reaction.

He looked her in the eye and nodded slowly as he put

the name together with the story he'd heard about the Cahills. Expert as she was at reading reactions in strangers' faces when they heard her name, Jane could see nothing but warmth in this man's eyes. She relaxed.

Beau Smith turned and opened the Bronco's tailgate. "I'll get this inside for you." Together they carried in the four cartons and five paper bags. When it was all piled on the kitchen floor he said, "Now don't tell me you're planning on staying out here. Not tonight anyway, not in this weather." He motioned toward the broken windows and defunct stove. "Come on home with me for the night, and I'll give you a hand tomorrow, getting the place weather-tight."

Jane was tempted, but only for an instant. A cold evening alone looked better to her than a warm one with people she didn't know. "Thanks, but I'll be okay. I can get the fireplace going now."

"It'll be down in the teens tonight," he warned. "Better come on home with me. My wife would disown me if I went off and left you here like this."

But Jane shook her head. "I plan to live here alone from now on and take care of myself, so I might as well start now. But thanks anyway, and thanks for bringing my stuff."

He frowned and pondered her, scratching his bearded jaw. "How old are you, if I may ask?"

"Seventeen."

"How come you're not in school?"

"I graduated yesterday. Midterm." Extra classes all last year, and summer school, and no elective subjects, just

16

what she needed to get the diploma six precious months earlier. No gowned ceremony, no graduation photographs, or gifts, or parties. But then she wouldn't have had those things in June either, and their lack was less noticeable at a midterm graduation.

Beau Smith leaned back against the table and crossed his arms over his barrel chest and cocked his head to stare at her. "So what are you going to do out here? You're not thinking of living here permanently, I trust."

She nodded. Looked him in the eye. Dared him to object.

He shook one hand as though he'd touched something hot. "They sure don't make teen-aged girls like they did in my day. Well, listen, if I can't talk you into coming back with me, at least I'll help you get that fireplace going. You got any wood? Matches?"

With a torn-up paper bag and twigs and sticks from outside the back door, they had a small fire snapping in the hearth in minutes. Jane hadn't known enough to cover the fireplace's opening before she cleaned the chimney, so soot and chunks of creosote lay thick over the end of the bedroom and had to be boot-scraped into a pile before they could get at the fireplace. But the chimney drew immediately and the small fire began warming the room. Jane stared into it, transfixed. Everything was going to work out. The fire proved it. With the fire going and a friendly neighbor beside her, images of ghosts receded and disappeared.

Together they carried in several armloads of wood. Then, assured that she had all she needed, Beau Smith left with a promise to check on her tomorrow. She closed the door on him with gratitude for his help, and for his leaving.

Working quickly because of the dimming light, she emptied one of the cardboard cartons, cut it into eight-by-teninch pieces, and taped them over the broken panes in the windows, using the tough strapping tape she'd brought. More tape covered cracks in three other panes. She smiled with the satisfaction of having shut the cold night out of her home.

For months Jane had gone to bed at night with paper and pen and sat up in the circle of her reading lamp making lists. What she would need for survival, how much it would cost, how long the $600 would last. She'd spent hours searching through garage sales for items on her list: scissors, dishes, cooking utensils, warm blankets, strapping tape, two battery-operated fluorescent camping lanterns, thirty paperback novels at ten cents apiece.

By the light of a fluorescent lantern she opened a can of corned beef hash, heated it in a pan in the fireplace, and ate it in the rocking chair beside the fire. Except for the snapping of the fire and the creak of her chair, her world was still. No television racket, no muted traffic noises from outside, no voices.

She began wishing she'd included a portable radio on her list. But it hadn't seemed important then.

She set down her plate and rested her head against the rocker's high back. Now that she was still she could hear the faint whistle of wind against the chimney cap and a distant barking of fox or dog. Peace came gradually, against the ripples of excitement and fear; peace eased the knots in her stomach and loosened her fingers.

After a while she was able to spread the mattress with all of her blankets, ease out of her boots, and climb into her bed in socks and jeans and sweatshirt. She lay tensely at first, an intruder on this bed.

But the wind whistled companionably in the chimney cap; she faded into sleep.

THREE

The next two days Jane worked harder and more joyously than she had ever worked before. She hauled water from the spring in garage-sale buckets, heated it in a pan in the fireplace, and scrubbed the cabin clean. She pried six of the rabbit cages loose from the barn wall and heaved them outside into the weak winter sun to scrub and disinfect them with stiff, blue-cold fingers. She found the missing length of stovepipe in a corner of the barn but couldn't get it into position single-handed. Reluctantly she set it aside until Beau Smith had time to help her.

In the long grass behind the barn she made an exciting discovery: the old jeep. All the tires were flat, the body was badly rusted, and the seats showed mouse damage, but it offered hope that someday, when she could afford tires and repairs, she might have transportation.

On the evening of the second day she opened her worn

copy of the American Rabbit Breeders Association's monthly magazine to the classified ads, found the ad she'd circled months ago, and wrote the letter she'd dreamed about. "Please send me five New Zealand Whites: one young breeding-quality buck, one good young doe bred to a different buck, three good young does ready to breed. Check enclosed, ship as soon as possible."

The check wasn't enclosed yet, but it would be as soon as she went to Prosper in the morning with the Smiths on their weekly shopping trip. When Beau had come to check on her the morning after her arrival, he'd left instructions about the shopping trip. They went to Prosper every Monday morning at about nine and would watch for her as they passed her road. If she wanted to ride along and do her town errands, she just needed to be waiting when they passed. Prosper, he told her, had a small branch bank, a decent-sized grocery store, a church, and a hardware store, and on Mondays the mobile library van was parked on Main Street from ten till two.

The four-mile trip to Prosper the next morning had the taste of adventure for Jane. Silently she chided herself for getting excited about a shopping trip to a tiny town. But it was her town now.

At the bank she opened a checking account and deposited her money. Carefully she wrote her first check for $150 for her five pedigreed rabbits, then crossed the street to the Post Office and mailed the order. There! It was on its way, the beginning of the Cahill Rabbitry. Only $480 in the bank now. The figure made her uneasy. She walked through the grocery-store aisles, passing up the Coke and potato chips

21

and Hershey bars she yearned for, and bought instead peanut butter, crackers, sandwich bread.

On the drive home, because she couldn't stand not to tell someone, Jane said, "I ordered my rabbits this morning. A buck and four does, from the top breeder in Arkansas."

"Rabbits," Mrs. Smith said. She was a tiny woman, who looked as though her dress size hadn't changed in forty years. Her hair was unbelievably black, her lipstick harshly red, but her eyes and voice were kind. Jane liked her as instinctively as she'd liked Beau. "You going to raise rabbits, are you?"

Jane nodded.

"Any money in that?" Beau asked politely, with an air of humoring her.

"Some. Not a whole lot, but I won't need much to live on, and I can always eat the ones I don't sell."

"Who you going to sell to?"

"A company in Rogers. It's a great big company that processes rabbit meat. My aunt used to work for them. They buy rabbits live. They come around on a regular route, and their buying truck is in Prosper twice a month. I checked it all out before I came down here."

"But how do you know they'll buy your rabbits, dear?" Marian asked.

"I talked to the buyer in Rogers. He said they buy New Zealand Whites or Californians or a few other breeds, fifty cents a pound live weight when the rabbits are three to four pounds, which is usually at about eight weeks of age. I guess they always have a big demand—they sell to grocery stores all over the country—so the guy I talked to said I wouldn't need to worry, they always bought."

Beau frowned as he drove. "Fifty cents a pound isn't a whole lot. Can you make a profit at that rate? That's only a couple of dollars a rabbit. How much are you paying for these you ordered today?"

"Well, thirty dollars apiece, but good breeding stock always costs more. And every book I read said to start with top-quality breeding stock, so I'm getting pedigreed and registered."

"Well," Beau shrugged, "I guess you know what you're doing." His tone showed doubt.

He drove the Bronco cautiously over the rocks of Jane's road. "You ought to call the county and have them run a grader over this road for you. They'll do it."

Jane shook her head. "I can't afford anything."

"I don't think they'd charge. I'm pretty sure this would be considered a county road. The county has to maintain it if anyone's living on it. I'll give them a call for you and ask, okay? Who owns the property?"

"I do. In trust till I'm of legal age, but it's in my name."

"Not your . . . mother?" His voice trailed away in awareness of the sensitivity of the subject.

Jane's jaw tightened. "There's a law that you can't benefit financially from a criminal act. My mother . . . murdered . . . my father, so she couldn't inherit from him." The words hung in the air, too powerful to be left ringing there. She hurried to cover them. "The place was hers before they got married, but he made her put it in his name, so it came down to me." She didn't want to talk about this. These people were too new to her, and too important.

Marian reached back from the front seat and patted

23

Jane's hand and said nothing. It was the right thing to do. Jane's stomach knot eased.

They'd had a hamburger lunch in town, Beau's treat, so he and Marian spent the afternoon at the house in the clearing. Beau and Jane wrestled the stovepipe into place after they'd scraped clean the whole pipe from stove to chimney top. While Jane swept up the mess, Beau wired together the sagging oven door, and Marian wandered around outside.

As they worked Beau answered Jane's questions. He told her that he and Marian had moved to Prosper four years ago, from Kirksville, Missouri, where he had been an engineer in a small hydraulics plant and Marian had taught fifth grade. They'd taken early retirement and had chosen Prosper because another family from their church back home had retired here. They had one son, Bob, who lived in St. Louis, worked as an aircraft maintenance engineer, and had the three cutest and smartest children in the history of the human race.

"What do you do with your time?" Jane asked, leaning on her broom.

"Fish, just like I dreamed about all those years in the plant back home. Putter around the place. Watch television. Get in Marian's way and drive her nuts. Oh, we have a pretty good time. We go to a lot of craft shows in the summer—Marian does some beautiful china painting, so we enjoy that—and then we have a lot of company in the summertime, too. Anybody that lives in a place like this is going to have a lot of friends dropping in from up north on vacation trips. And then we're pretty active in the church here. Saturday night bingo parties and the like."

24

Jane began to get a sense of two societies moving around her on separate planes: the natives, like herself, and the northern retirees who moved into the pastel bungalows that lined the highways. It was as though her territory had been invaded by a gentle tide of outsiders, benevolent couples like Beau and Marian who might accept her more easily than her own people. To the natives, shootings like the Cahills', between husbands and wives, were much more common than they would be to the Smiths but more deeply felt, stirring passions that were rooted in another century.

To the Smiths, Jane perceived, she was the unfortunate victim of a family tragedy. To Doyle and Marlyce Cahill she was an inseparable part of a violence that had robbed them of one of their own, and as such she would never be forgiven.

Marian joined them as the fire in the repaired stove began to catch hold and throw warmth. The three of them stood around the stove, hands out to catch the heat.

Marian looked around at the comfortless house and said, "I just hate to think of you living out here all alone, no plumbing or electricity or company. It's not the life for a young girl like you. You ought to be going off to college, enjoying yourself. You're so young to be turning yourself into a hermit. What are you going to do for boyfriends in a place like this?"

Jane thought, *Same thing I've always done. Without. It doesn't matter where I live with a face like mine. There aren't going to be boyfriends for me anyhow. Easier out here, where there aren't any possibilities. No chances, no disappointments.* She smiled and shook her head at Marian's question, and the Smiths let it drop.

The house was silent except for the crackling of the fire in the stove. Through her jacket Jane could feel the beginning of comfortable warmth combatting the chill drafts from the cardboarded windows.

Beau's glance followed her own to the windows. Briskly he said, "Well, at least let me fix those windows for you. You can't live through the winter with that situation. What are they, eight-by-ten panes?"

"Yes, but I can't afford—"

"Don't worry about that. I'll put 'em on my bill at the hardware store and you can pay me back whenever. It won't amount to much anyway." He went through both rooms, counting cracked and missing panes. "And what are you doing about firewood? That little bit out back isn't going to last long, with the stove going."

"I thought I'd get a saw."

"Chain saw? No, I guess you'd want something cheaper. A good sharp D-saw would do the job. I've got one you can borrow for now, if you want."

When they finally left, Jane was equally grateful for their help and for their leaving.

For the next six days Jane worked from sunup till dark on the woodpile. Beau had come and puttied in the new windowpanes, so with the cold kept out and both fireplace and stove going full-time, the house was finally comfortably warm. She was able to sleep in sweatshirt only and walk the linoleum floors in slippers instead of boots. But the stove and fireplace ate voraciously into the last of the old woodpile.

26

With Beau's D-shaped hand saw and an ancient wheel-barrow from the barn, Jane made excursions into the woods beyond the clearing and cut up stove-lengths of fallen branches and the trunks of small dead trees. It was slow, laborious work, and it became increasingly painful as blisters rose and broke and rose again in the palm of her sawing hand. The weather turned cloudy and colder, barely above zero in the mornings and damply raw. Each day she burned almost half of what she cut, so the stockpile grew depressingly slowly. After the second day she let the fire go out in the bedroom and didn't light it until she came in for supper. After that the stockpile gained a little faster.

Meals were sketchy and housecleaning nonexistent during those outdoor days. It didn't matter that the evenings were long and dark and unlit by electricity; she went to bed exhausted after supper and slept deeply, without remembered dreams. If there were ghosts in the bedroom with her, they didn't keep her awake.

During those days, tensions began to melt from her body, tensions so old and ingrained in her life that she hardly knew they were there until they eased away. She chewed more slowly, unhunched her shoulders unaware.

The next Monday Beau and Marian did their shopping in the larger and more distant Fayetteville, because Marian had a doctor's appointment there. Jane rode along and bought her first fifty-pound bag of rabbit pellets at the feed mill. It excited her to smell it and heave it into the Bronco. One step closer to the reality of the Cahill Rabbitry. The five dollars she paid for it was almost painless.

But the grocery store took another twelve and that was

not painless. Again she bought the cheapest, most filling things she could think of: tea, cereal, sandwich bread, and peanut butter.

A few days later, when the woodpile had grown to a size that warranted a day off, she went walking down the highway in the opposite direction from Prosper, just to see what was there. Beau had mentioned a small store and gas station a mile down the road past his place, and she was running low on matches.

The day was sunny and warmer than it had been. She unzipped her jacket and strode along the blacktop, whistling through her teeth. Ten days of cutting and hauling wood had begun to toughen her muscles so that her legs carried her tirelessly.

She found the store-station at the bottom of a long hill, beside an old iron bridge that spanned the White River. The store was a sagging mustard-yellow structure with a pair of elderly gas pumps in front and a large cat, yellow-and-mustard-striped to match the building, stretched across the doorway. She lifted the tip of her tail as Jane stepped over her but didn't bother to move.

There was only one person inside, a large middle-aged woman on a stool behind the cash register. She looked at Jane with interest but, like the cat, didn't bother to get up. "Mornin'," she said.

Jane sensed that the woman knew who she was. "Morning."

The store was one small room cluttered with souvenir caps, fishing supplies, dusty packets of potato chips and corn curls. A cooler in the back held Popsicles and ice-cream sandwiches.

The woman heaved herself off the stool and leaned across the counter. "Just as a guess, I'd say you was Jane Cahill, am I right?"

Jane looked at her cautiously and nodded. "How did you know that?"

The woman shrugged. "You came on foot, from up the hill, and I heard you'd moved back in up there. I'm Iva Oliphant. Just call me Iva. How you making out up there? I heard you was going into rabbits."

Jane shrugged and turned away to look for matches. "Yeah, kind of."

"Your dad had a good many rabbits up there at one time, didn't he?"

Jane turned and looked at the woman, over a stack of T-shirts that said, "Fishermen have a better line."

"Did you know him . . . then?"

"Oh, honey, I been here since the dawn of time. I know everybody in this county and everything about them. I even knew you when you were knee high to a toad, don't you remember? You used to come in here with your ma."

Jane shook her head. The memory was there, but so faint it was almost gone, like so many of her memories of that life. Blocked out, she figured, by the things that were too painful to remember.

Iva shifted her weight from elbow to elbow and said, "Yessir, your dad used to sell dressed rabbits to lots of folks around here. My husband used to buy from him every now and again. Good meat, those rabbits. We can't afford it in the stores, it's too expensive, but if you're going to be selling any dressed meat, you let me know, hear?"

Jane nodded but said nothing about the fear she had that

she wouldn't be able to kill and skin a rabbit, even for her own table, much less on a larger scale to sell to others. That was why she'd chosen the least profitable end of rabbit raising, the selling of live animals to a meat processor.

She picked up a box of matches and was digging out the money to pay for them when a thought struck her.

"Say, you don't happen to know what ever happened to my pa's rabbits after . . . he died, do you? I never even thought about it till now."

Iva pondered. "Well, as I recall, Eldon Shaffley from over by Mountaintop come and got those rabbits. I remember him saying he didn't want them starving to death out there with nobody to take care of them. He knew your dad."

"Mountaintop. Is that very far from here?" Jane's mind raced.

"Nah, ten, twelve miles south. Eldon lives right on the highway. You can't miss it if you was thinking about going down there."

Jane thanked her and left the store, stepping over the cat. She stood forming her thoughts for a moment, then turned south.

She found Eldon Shaffley skinning rabbits behind his barn, which, like Jane's barn, was filled with rabbit cages. Unlike Jane's, his cages were alive with mounded white forms. On the back wall of the barn several rabbit carcasses were hung upside down, beheaded and dripping blood. The bent and toothless Mr. Shaffley was pulling a hide down off of one carcass, like shedding a sweater, Jane thought.

She told him who she was and, in a matter-of-fact way, why she had come. "I figured since you took over my pa's herd when he died, you owe me some rabbits."

The man chewed on it for a few minutes while he worked globs of fat off the inside-out hide with the ball of his thumb. Finally he said, "I reckon I do, at that. I tried to get aholt of somebody from the family at the time, but there wasn't no one around, and I didn't want them rabbits starving to death. I don't have as big a herd as I used to. My heart's getting a little dickey on me, so I been cutting back. But I reckon I could spare you, what would you say, twenty-five, thirty nice young ones? That be fair?"

Jane nodded. They shook on the deal and agreed on a day next week when he could deliver the rabbits. She left and began the long hitchhike home, with figures spinning in her head.

Instead of the expected four does to start her herd with, there were going to be twenty-nine. She shouted wild hoorays inside and began to multiply: *twenty-nine does times five litters a year if I push them, times an average of six young to a litter, times two dollars apiece from the Freez-Fine buyer. . . .*

Riches!

FOUR

Within a week Jane was a rabbit breeder. Scrubbed and disinfected cages stretched the length of the barn, with hunched white mounds of fur peering out red-eyed at her as she walked past checking feed hoppers and water dishes. She wrestled open the large south doors of the barn on warm afternoons to let in fresh air and sunshine and to lighten the barn so that she could admire her stock.

The five expensive pedigreed rabbits were noticeably bigger and finer than the thirty from Shaffley, well worth the expense, she decided. With young bucks from the pedigreed herd she could upgrade the quality of the other stock and still have plenty to sell to the Freez-Fine buyer.

February came, and abruptly Jane found herself fighting dark moods. The first excitement of settling into her new life was past. The little house had become hers, inhabited less and less by unsettling memories of her parents. She was comfortable in those two shabby rooms in a way that she had never experienced before, but the comfort became accepted; she noticed it less and less as the days passed.

The woodpile was a constant job, but one that no longer required thought. It required mornings in the woods with her D-saw and wheelbarrow, but it left her mind free. In the afternoons she puttered in the barn watching the rabbits, or repairing cages for future use, or craning for peeks at the recently kindled litter from the pedigreed doe that had been shipped already bred. The eight pink mouselike babies slept in a knot within their nest box, blanketed by fur their mother had pulled out of her own belly for them. They were exciting in their prospects but nothing to look at yet.

When she could find nothing to do in the barn, Jane spent afternoon hours on her bed with her feet toasting toward the fire, reading romance novels from the Prosper bookmobile or figuring on scraps of paper.

Both occupations were ultimately depressing. The romance novels simply had nothing to do with Jane Cahill. They were a habit left over from high school, and even then they had been a mute attempt at being like the other girls in her class. Now they made her uncomfortably aware of the existence she had chosen for herself and the paucity of human love it was going to offer.

The figuring on scraps of paper added to the uneasiness she was beginning to feel about her chosen life-style. With the bonanza of the Shaffley rabbits the figures looked much better than they had originally, but they were still grim. In the six weeks since she'd come here, Jane's money had faded at the rate of about twenty dollars a week for subsistence-level groceries, and now an additional five a week for rabbit pellets. The total in the checkbook stood at $310 and falling.

And that was just for food. In the fall there would be the $420 for property taxes, formerly paid by Doyle and added to her debt to him. She had no hospitalization insurance now that she was no longer in Doyle Cahill's household. She couldn't depend on the Smiths forever for hauling rabbit feed and groceries, and that might mean several hundred dollars for getting the jeep running, and more for insurance, license plates, and gas. Even the seeds and starter plants for this spring's garden were going to make a visible dent in her money.

Over and over she figured: *Thirty breeding does, five litters a year if I push them, six salable babies per litter, not counting the ones I keep for replacement breeders, that makes nine hundred rabbits to sell, at two dollars a rabbit, total yearly income of $1,800. After property taxes, a little over a hundred a month to live on. Not enough.*

Okay, double the number of breeding does, triple it, say a hundred does. I could live on that if I had to, but I'd have to sink a lot into material to build that many cages, and there isn't room for that many in the barn.

Am I really sure this is the way I want to spend my life?

She thought about all the other options. College. A hundred careers to choose from, any one of which would provide her with a comfortable living. But of course there was no money for college, not without full scholarships, and her grades weren't that good. She simply hadn't worked hard

34

enough at it to maintain that kind of grade level; there had been too much peripheral unhappiness distracting her.

And she'd instinctively shrunk away from the idea of college campuses teeming with beautiful, confident girls, handsome young men who would look past her. . . .

Am I hiding out here? Am I such a coward that I can't face life like everybody else? At a big college no one would know or care about my family background. I'd be judged just for myself.

Maybe that's what I'm scared of.

To try to clarify her thoughts she projected herself ten years into the future: *If I went to college and became a vet, in ten years I'd just be getting out, going to work in some small-animal clinic in some city. I'd probably gain some self-confidence along the way, but I'd still be homely as a mud fence. I'd work long hours in a pet hospital, having to deal with clients and office girls and other vets, having to compete, having to be around people all day and get up to an alarm clock every morning of my life.*

Ten years from now, if I stay here, I'd probably have the rabbit business built up to some sort of livable income or else found some other way of keeping body and soul together without having to leave this place. I'd have the house fixed up prettier and more comfortably, I'd have the jeep or something like it so I wouldn't have to bum rides. I'd have friends in the neighborhood, like the Smiths and Iva. I'd be used to living alone, probably spoiled to it so I wouldn't ever live any other way. If somebody did come along to marry I probably wouldn't want to because I'd be too used to living every minute for myself.

The joy of her aloneness was growing daily more evident to Jane. The tiny luxuries of waking in the mornings, lying in bed until she'd had time to plan her day, eating what she wanted for every meal, within the limits of her budget, instead of wordlessly accepting whatever Marlyce fixed, eating when she was hungry, not when someone else decreed that it was mealtime, being in control of her day. That, she thought, was the key. Control. She had to listen to no one's noise but her own. She worked hard, but she worked according to her own decisions, and for her own direct benefit.

No, she thought, *I could never shoehorn myself into college life now, or even a job in town. This is me. This life fits my nature.*

And with that realization she would temporarily cease to worry about the money or the fact that she was living in a way that everyone else thought was wrong for her.

Everyone except Iva.

On a Monday afternoon in late February, Jane sat in a cluttered little living room behind Iva's store. She had walked down after her trip to town with Beau and Marian just to talk to Iva, who was becoming an unexpected friend. When leaning over the counter became uncomfortable, they moved to the back room and sank into the pair of platform rockers on either side of Iva's wood stove, with mugs of hot chocolate to warm them.

"I don't know," Jane said, looking down at the brown grains of undissolved instant cocoa floating in her mug. "Every time I'm around Beau and Marian they make me feel like, you know, I'm making some terrible mistake liv-

ing the way I am. They're good-hearted as they can be,
but..."

Iva nodded, setting her jowls in motion. Her gray hair
was cut as short as a man's and her neck sported several
large moles. She wore loose denim slacks and a plaid flannel shirt and boots that laced up out of sight.

"They probably figure you're throwing your life away if
you don't get married. There's still people in the world
who'll try to tell you any marriage at all is better than none
at all. Better than growing old alone." She snorted.

Jane tipped her head to one side and studied Iva. "So
what do you think? How long have you been living alone?"

"Fourteen years come July. My husband died of cat-
scratch disease not two months after we bought this place."

"Did you love him a lot? Was it hard for you to live
alone after being married all that time?"

Iva chuckled and sniffed. "I tell you, Janey, living alone
wasn't a whole hell of a lot different from living with
Harold. We sort of went our own ways, even when we was
young. Oh, we had some good times in them young years,
but he was always trying this and that, trying to make a
living without having to work any more than necessary. He
ran trout lines in the river summers and did a little farming,
raised a few head of beef cattle but never enough to
amount to anything. I more or less supported us even when
he was alive. Old Harold was a failer by nature. Failed at
this, that, and the other. He'd have failed at running this
store if he'd of lived longer.

"Tell you the truth, I've got along a good bit better on
my own than I did with him, not that I'd have wished him

37

dead, you understand. Naturally I missed his company at first, but I got over it."

"You don't mind . . . growing old alone then?"

Iva laughed a deep belly laugh. "Oh, hell, I been young alone and that wasn't so bad. Being old alone is no big deal. Everybody's afraid of it. Me, I kind of like it. Not that I don't like people, or value my friends. I just don't feel any need to live in somebody else's pocket."

"I read something somewhere." Jane closed her eyes to remember the exact words. "It was something like, 'Loneliness is poverty of self. Solitude is richness of self.'"

"Well, there's truth in that," Iva stated. "If a person likes herself, she don't mind spending time in her own company. I figure when I talk to myself I got an intelligent audience." She laughed again.

"And no arguments," Jane added.

"You said a mouthful."

Jane grew quietly thoughtful. "But what about selfishness? I mean, people aren't supposed to live just for themselves. You have to, you know, give to others. Don't you? Like the song says about people who need people are the luckiest people in the world."

Iva snorted. "What's lucky about need? Seems like to me, the needy ones are the ones that other folks wipe their feet on. If you're strong, in yourself," she chose her words carefully, "then you can like people or love them or whatever, not because you have some sort of need that that person can fulfill, but just plain like them for themselves. That seems like a better way, to me."

Jane pondered.

"What I mean," Iva went on, "look at all the young people your age that jump into some dang-fool marriage. Like I did. They might tell themselves it's because they're head over heels in love, but usually that's not it, not really. It's because maybe their folks didn't give them enough love so they're *needy,* see, and they go looking for it from somebody else. Or a young girl gets married because she gets out of school, takes a look at the world, and gets all intimidated by things like making her living, learning how to handle money, or keep her car running, or what-all. Some guy comes along and says 'I'll take care of you forever,' and she gets to leaning on him, figures she *needs* him to help her get through life, and bang, you got the beginnings of a shaky marriage. She outgrows him or he gets tired of having her hang on him. Maybe he married her in the first place because he was at a time in his life when he *needed* somebody to look up to him and hang on to him. And then he grows up some, and his needs change. See what I mean? They latch on to each other out of temporary need, not any kind of genuine love for that individual. The needs change as they get older and the whole thing falls apart."

"So what's your answer?" Jane asked, with a glimmer of humor.

"Wellsir, if I was God and running the world, I'd try to make it so everybody, men and women, had to live alone for a while, take care of themselves, support themselves, learn their own strengths, if you know what I mean. Then they'd be a lot more likely to marry for the right reasons, and stay married."

"Or not marry at all?"

39

"Or not marry at all. I truly believe that's the best answer for some people."

"Me, do you think?"

Iva narrowed her eyes and studied Jane. "I couldn't say, till I know you better. You may be cut out to be a solitary, all right."

Jane was silent for a long moment. "And you don't think that's necessarily an unhappy life, going through it alone, living alone? Being a hermitess, as Beau calls me?"

Iva waved her away with a sweep of her hand. "Don't ask me to make your life decisions for you, girl. I don't want that responsibility. Follow your own gut instincts. Don't listen to Beau Smith or me, either one."

Jane lay in bed that night, hands clasped behind her head, staring into the fire.

Gut instincts. Her gut instincts were loud and clear. Stay here in this hidden clearing, relish her aloneness, build a life here.

Instincts . . . or cowardice?

FIVE

In March came the fragrant Ozark spring and a daily deepening joy. Does kindled litters of naked pink mites that grew into white fluffballs scooting about their cages. Jane spent hours watching them, counting them, making records of them in her notebook, and readying additional cages to hold them after weaning.

She spent even longer stretches of time in the square of garden behind the house. As soon as the frost was out of the ground, she began digging with a rusted spade from the barn. Every thrust of the spade was frustrated by collision with the sandy-red rocks that peeked through and lurked below the poor, thin soil. Most of the rocks were small enough to toss aside; it was their persistence rather than their size that was disheartening. Although the garden was just thirty feet square, it took her more than two weeks of afternoons to spade it, rock-free, six inches deep.

The discarded rocks she piled in a miniature fence

around the garden's edge. It was low enough to step over easily, too low to keep out animals from the woods, but it looked good to Jane—neat and somehow satisfying, an enemy conquered.

By this time the rabbit manure was inches thick on the barn floor. Jane shoveled and hauled and dumped load after load of it onto the garden, then dug it in till the soil was mixed almost half and half with the manure. And still, every time she turned under a shovelful, new small rocks came to the surface.

She planted packets of seeds, chunks of seed potatoes, tiny tomato, squash, and melon plants, then spent more afternoons hauling endless buckets of water from the spring to soak the infant plants.

Days were pleasantly warm by now. She left the doors and windows open and let the fires go out in the daytime. The clearing became green and, more gradually, so did the woods. The creek grew full and sibilant, sparkling over its rocky bed. At the edge of the woods, serviceberries opened their showy white blossoms, dogwood trees bloomed pale purple, and in the sparse grass, blue Johnny-jump-ups nodded. Every time she came out of the house or walked into the woods Jane felt an airy sense of well-being.

One day in early April, Jane was surprised by the roar, and later the appearance, of a county road maintainer scraping its way slowly along her road, its giant blade smoothing lumps into gullies and leveling both. In the clearing the driver waved to her, maneuvered the mammoth yellow machine around in a U-turn, and disappeared into the trees, roaring and scraping away into silence. After that, the road was usable by ordinary cars, not just Beau's four-wheel-drive Bronco.

A few days later it was used. On a Sunday afternoon, when Jane had settled on a blanket beside the creek for an hour of reading, a strange station wagon drove in. A nicely dressed older couple stepped out and approached, with plastic garbage bags in their hands.

"We were talking to Marian Smith after church today," the man said, "and she told us you were raising rabbits. We've been looking for rabbit manure for our garden. Suppose you could sell us some?"

The deal was made, two dollars a bag, and Jane shoveled five bags full for them. They lingered to admire her garden, the clearing, the baby bunnies. The woman said things Jane was coming to expect. "You don't live out here all alone surely? Nice young girl like you? Aren't you afraid? Don't you get lonesome?"

And beside the garden: "Isn't this Arkansas soil dreadful? We moved down here from Illinois when Gerald retired. We sure wish we could have brought some of that good black soil down here with us. You should have seen the garden we had back home. Where are you from?"

"Right here," Jane told them. A flicker of interest passed between the man and woman. Their social circle included only other retired Northerners like themselves and the Smiths. Natives were a novelty to them.

As they left, Jane thanked them and called out a reminder to tell their gardening friends about her manure supply. "Best thing you can use on a garden," she said, and they agreed.

After that several other cars and pickups found their way down the rock road to the clearing, and for a few weeks Jane's groceries were paid for entirely by rabbit manure.

"You could say I'm dining on manure," she joked to Iva.

"You could, but who'd want to?" They laughed together.

A week before Easter, on an impulse, Jane called a Fayetteville pet shop from the Smiths' phone and asked if they would be interested in stocking some bunnies for Easter pets. Yes, the manager said, if she could deliver twenty healthy just-weaned babies by the next day, he would pay five dollars apiece for them. Cheering inside, Jane agreed. The next day was Marian's doctor's appointment in Fayetteville, so transportation was no problem.

Carefully Jane selected twenty newly weaned bunnies, put them in the shipping cages her pedigreed animals had come in, and delivered them to the pet shop. One hundred dollars, just like that. She exulted.

The store manager seemed pleased with the clean, healthy bunnies and said that they could probably use a few more from time to time. He took Jane's name and the Smiths' phone number and said he'd be in touch.

On the ride home Jane silently figured: If only there was enough of a market to sell all her offspring to pet shops for five dollars apiece, instead of two dollars apiece to Freez-Fine. . . . A hundred breeding does times five litters a year times six live babies a litter times five dollars . . . $15,000 a year. That was almost like a real job with a genuine salary. Maybe enough for a running jeep, electricity for the house, and an occasional can of Coke.

Then reality dimmed the dream. Before she could hope

to establish pet-shop markets, she would have to have the jeep running. She couldn't ask Beau and Marian to drive her that far, that often. The hundred dollars in her denim purse would have to go for groceries and rabbit feed, with no more than maybe twenty or thirty left over by the time she made her first Freez-Fine sale, still two weeks away.

"I hate being broke all the time," she said suddenly, forgetting she was with people.

Beau and Marian laughed. "I thought you were rolling in wealth," he teased.

"Not enough."

"Well, you're not alone in that boat, honey," Marian said with a chuckle.

Sure, she can say that, Jane thought. *They've got two Social Security checks and their retirement funds from their jobs. Plenty to support themselves and their cars, to buy frozen gourmet dinners if they don't feel like cooking, and trips to Silver Dollar City every time relatives come down to visit.*

That afternoon she walked down to visit Iva and to blow a precious fifty cents on a cold can of Coke from Iva's machine. She was amazed to find that, after four months of drinking only springwater, tea, and sometimes Iva's hot chocolate, the carbonated soft drink tasted gassy and harsh and gave her hiccups.

"I guess I've lost my taste for the luxuries of life," she said drily and gave the rest of the can to Iva.

"Stuff's no good for you anyway," Iva said, tipping up the can and finishing it off.

They sat side by side on the wooden bench in front of the

45

store while the cat, Bag Lady, wove in and out among their legs, stropping herself against them. Three of her half-grown kittens chased grasshoppers across the broken cement by the gas pump.

"Iva," Jane said thoughtfully.

"Present."

"Do you know anyone around here who could take a look at my jeep and see how much it needs to get it running, and not charge me for looking at it? I know it needs tires and probably a battery, and I can't afford anything right now, really, but if I could get it running I might be able to sell some more baby rabbits to pet shops. Trouble is, I'd have to go probably as far as Springfield and Harrison and Fort Smith in order to find enough pet shops, and I can't do that without wheels."

"I'll come take a look at it for you if you want."

Jane's eyes widened. "Can you do stuff like that?"

"Sure. I'm your basic renaissance woman, remember? I can do anything."

"She said modestly," Jane teased.

"Listen, toots, you stir it and stump it and blow your own trumpet. Ain't nobody else going to blow it for you."

"Good then." Jane grinned. "When could you look at the jeep?"

"How's about now? I think we can hold off this mad rush of business for an hour or so." They looked up the road and down it. The last car had passed half an hour before, and the last customer three hours before that. Iva set the *Gone for emergency call* sign in the door and motioned Jane toward her pickup. Then she paused.

"Why don't you take one of them kittens along? You could use a cat in your barn, couldn't you? Keep the mice and rats down?"

Jane hesitated. "I can't afford cat food."

"Table scraps and hunting ought to be enough, at least till you start butchering a few rabbits for your own table. A cat can get lots of good out of the parts you don't want. Go ahead, take one."

With pleasure Jane selected and scooped up the biggest of the kittens, a tortoiseshell so dark she was almost solid black, with just traces of gold on her face and legs. *Company would be wonderful*, Jane thought. Then, *Am I going to turn into the classic neurotic old maid with her houseful of cats? Oh well, might as well be strange one way as another.*

Iva pried up the creaking hood of the jeep and began banging battery terminals and hose connections with her wrench. She pulled out the battery, put in water and acid, and attached it to the charger on the back of her pickup. Then she went to work replacing sparkplugs and rotted rubber hoses.

"I can't afford much of anything," Jane warned two or three times. Iva just grunted. She poured springwater into the radiator, knocked the remains of a squirrel's nest out of the air filter, and poured a little gas into the tank from the emergency can in the pickup. Then, while the battery was charging, she and Jane walked around the clearing looking at the house, garden, and rabbits. They settled the kitten in the kitchen and had a cup of tea, the only hospitality Jane

47

could afford to offer. Then they went back outside and replaced the battery in the jeep.

"It might or might not hold the charge," Iva warned, "and there might be other things wrong in there that I didn't spot. So don't be disappointed if it doesn't take right off."

Jane said with sudden dismay, "I forgot. I don't know where the key is."

They found the key. In the ignition. "It's been sitting here twelve years with the key in the ignition?" Jane said, amazed.

"Honest neighborhood," Iva said with a chuckle. "Either that or it wouldn't run. Makes them hard to steal, when they won't run. Well, here goes nothing." She climbed into the cracked and dusty driver's seat and turned the key. The motor ground.

"At least it made a noise," Jane said hopefully.

On the second try it caught, and ran.

"Yay-hoo!" Jane yelled, and Iva whooped and beat her palms against the steering wheel.

"I thought sure I'd have to get a new battery at the very least," Jane said, her voice rich with delight. "Now all it needs is tires."

Iva said, "You can get retreads for around twenty bucks apiece. They wouldn't last long on these rocks, but they'd do for a while if you didn't drive much."

Jane nodded. But eighty dollars . . . that was still a dream for the future. And there was the insurance, the registration, the license plates. One step forward, two steps back.

*   *   *

Two weeks later, in early May, the Cahill Rabbitry made its first sale to the Freez-Fine company, in the buyer's truck in the rear of the grocery store's parking lot, in Prosper. Jane had built carrying cages out of scraps of lumber and wire, in order to haul her fifty fryer-sized rabbits in the back of the Bronco.

The buyer's truck was large and solid-sided, with "Freez-Fine Rabbits, Rogers, Arkansas," lettered in white against the truck's dark green. Two other breeders were there waiting, smoking, visiting, while the young man within the truck weighed their rabbits and tallied the weights in his book. Beau and Marian excused themselves and walked away toward the grocery store.

The other two breeders were both men, both middle-aged and bent. They reminded Jane of Eldon Shaffley, and she wondered whether she would have to become old and bent to fit in with the crowd. She smiled and the men smiled back, mistaking her smile as intended for them.

She was secretly delighted to see that her rabbits looked at least as good as theirs. Better, in her opinion. And she had more of them.

When both men had left and it was her turn, the young man jumped down from the truck and helped her lift her crates up onto the floor of the truck.

"You've got quite a herd here," he said, looking directly at Jane for the first time and smiling. "I haven't seen you before, have I?"

She shook her head. She wanted to say something smooth, but her tongue went treacherously thick. He af-

fected her as all the self-assured high school boys had. He
had the smooth-skinned face, the curly blond hair, the
breezy manner that automatically made Jane's face ache
with its ugliness, made her want to turn away from him so
he couldn't see and judge and compare her with pretty
girls.

"Well," he said as he began lifting rabbits from her cages
into the cage on his scale, "I'm practically a stranger here
myself. I worked this route last summer, and I probably
will again this summer. This week I'm just home for a few
days. This is my dad's route in the winter, but I said I'd
take it for him today. He's got bursitis, and some days his
shoulders are really bad. And he likes to have his summers
off for fishing. We've got a cabin up on Beaver Lake."

"Do you go to college?" Jane managed.

"Yeah, at Cape Girardeau. Junior, in education. I'm
going to be a junior high football coach, so I'm getting
some education minors. It's so much easier to get a coach-
ing job if you can teach math or science, too, especially in
smaller schools. Where do you go?"

Jane shook her head.

"You're not in college? Sorry, you looked like the right
age. You out of high school? What do you do?"

"Raise rabbits," she said in a low voice.

"For a living?" He looked at her, surprised.

"Kind of a living, yeah."

"Wow. That's a switch."

"Why?"

"Well, I don't know. It doesn't seem like, well, you
know."

"Not very ordinary," she said wryly. "Not a suitable occupation for a young lady."

He laughed and shrugged and said, "Different strokes." He finished the weighing and picked up his record book. "Name?" She told him. "Address? Phone number? Measurements? Just kidding, don't get hostile."

"The address is Route Two, Prosper, no phone."

"And no measurements." He grinned wickedly. "Here you are, Miss Jane Cahill, two hundred forty pounds of fryers, one hundred twenty dollars. Don't blow it all in one place." He ripped the check from a large page of checks and handed it to her with a flourish.

She left him and wandered toward the grocery store, elated by the money and even more elated by the fact that she had been almost flirted with, by a college junior. A handsome one. Incredible.

Maybe life at the back of beyond didn't have to be entirely hermitish after all.

SIX

Jane's Eden had its serpents. As spring warmth became summer heat, scorpions grew active in the house's dark corners and copperheads slithered in the creek. Jane grew cautious when she waded in to bathe or wash her hair. Her eyes skimmed the path ahead when she walked to the spring or to woodcutting sites.

Ticks came from nowhere. After every trip into the woods she dropped her jeans and picked tiny seed ticks from her legs, checked her hair with probing strokes, and gritted her teeth to pull attached ticks from her scalp.

But these were small prices to pay, she thought, for the daily growing of an aspect new to her character. She was beginning to admire herself.

The self that she admired was visible in the house, now bright and tidy and comfortable; in the neat green rows of vegetables that were feeding her almost entirely now; in the four rust-red hens that she had bought with manure money and learned to care for from library books, and that were giving her scrambled-egg breakfasts, free. The admirable self was evident in the growing healthy rabbit herd and the growing figures in her checkbook, back up to six hundred again, with the jeep retread-shod and legalized and running.

With each solved problem, with each tiny advance in the quality of her life, Jane looked her inner self more squarely in the eye and smiled in recognition.

"I may not be gorgeous, but by God I can take care of myself."

When she talked to herself now it was with a sense of sharing with a friend. The cat, Urchin, was with her constantly and served as a listener, but Jane's comments were essentially aimed at herself, and this no longer struck her as a sign of oddity. She was becoming openly what she had always been in essence, her own best friend.

By early summer she was eating almost entirely from the garden. Peas and spinach and early tomatoes, beans and new potatoes and the first clusters of broccoli made up her meals, along with the two or three eggs a day from her hens, and rhubarb she discovered at the back of the clearing. Raspberries growing wild in the woods were her snacks and desserts.

From a library book she learned to can the green beans that came almost literally by the bushel, the rich rabbit manure having offset the poorness of the soil. She canned potatoes and tomatoes, made raspberry and rhubarb preserves. How-to books replaced the romance novels she got each week from the bookmobile. She had no time these days for romance novels, and no interest.

Beau and Marian worried about her diet. "You have to have meat," Beau insisted. "You don't want to lose your health, girl. There you are with a hundred rabbits in your barn and never a bite of meat passes your lips except when we feed you."

With the jeep running, Jane no longer went into Prosper with the Smiths on Mondays, but the three of them had developed the habit of Sunday dinner together at the Smiths' after Beau and Marian came home from church. Jane never accepted their invitations to church; twelve years of Doyle's insistence on church to offset her evil nature had soured her on Sunday mornings in a pew. Instead, on Sundays she went to the Smiths' compact green bungalow late in the morning and put the chicken in the oven, started the potatoes, set the table, and luxuriated in television, air conditioning, and instant water.

"I'll start butchering a few rabbits one of these days," she said more calmly than she felt. "And besides, I'm getting vegetable protein, and my eggs. Don't worry about me."

On the Fourth of July the Smiths insisted on including Jane in their plans. With the visiting son and daughter-in-law and grandchildren, they went to Beaver Lake for a fishing picnic aboard the Smiths' pontoon boat. The boat was broad and flat as a houseboat but had only a canopy roof and low side-railings. Its two long pontoons floated it gently on the lake's waves while Beau grilled steaks and made broad old jokes about his captain's status. The children yelled and chased around the deck and hung dangerously over the rails, taunting their parents.

Much as Jane appreciated the invitation and the family feeling of being included, and much as she enjoyed the day, she felt a distinct relief when she was finally able to leave the Smiths and drive her jeep up the green tunnel of her private road, into the serenity of her clearing.

By mid-July the rabbits were in full production and the breeding herd was up to fifty-three does, twelve of them from the good pedigreed stock. Litters were kindled with rabbity regularity, even though they fell a little short of her projected five litters a year, six young per litter. Some does failed to conceive and a few killed their newborn young, but others routinely produced eight or nine babies at three-month intervals, some every two months, breeding again while still nursing their young.

Every two weeks, on Freez-Fine day, Jane took a load of eight-week-old fryers to the teasing-eyed young man in the buyers' truck, Aaron Bruns. When he didn't have other breeders waiting, he kept her there talking, mostly about his life but with occasional curious questions about hers. Gradually she thawed toward him and began treating him almost as though he were a real person, not a handsome college man. So secretly that she hardly acknowledged it even to herself, those morning meetings with Aaron became the anticipated high point of her weeks.

On a Saturday evening in late July, Jane stood in the barn staring thoughtfully at the rows of rabbit cages, her record book in her arm. The cages were in a double row now, the old dim-wired ones on top and bright, new Jane-built cubicles below, with tin trays between to catch droppings and urine.

Most of the new cages were already occupied with young does and bucks from the pedigreed herd, waiting to reach breeding age and to replace the poorer Shaffley animals. It was only Shaffley offspring that she had been selling to Freez-Fine and, a few at a time, to pet shops in Fayetteville and Rogers.

Jane looked again at her herd record book to be sure. Three of the Shaffley does had failed to produce offspring at all, in spite of regular journeys to the bucks' cages and vigorous breedings. Each buck had produced with other does, so it was obvious that the problem lay with the three barren does themselves. From the length and yellowness of their teeth Jane suspected that these does were simply beyond breeding age.

Time to take them out of the herd and make room for younger, better replacements. Time to butcher them and eat them.

She shuddered.

"Well," she said to Urchin, who sat staring intently at a cageful of hopping bunnies, "we can't put it off any longer. Tomorrow is the day. I'll do all three of them at once and get it over with, and if I survive that, I'll know I can be a real rabbit breeder all the way. Even if I'm not a bent-over old geezer."

Urchin paid no attention. She was used to Jane's monologues and ignored them unless they promised food.

"I know what. I'll invite the Smiths and Iva for Sunday

dinner tomorrow. How would that be? Yes. I like that idea. I can pay back my social obligations and force myself to go through with the butchering, too. If I invite them I'll have to have something to feed them, right?"

In the remaining half hour of usable daylight she moved about the barn, finding and gathering the tools she would need. Her father's old knives were there, and a whetstone to sharpen them. On the back wall of the barn, outside, were nails with loops of wire hanging from them. Everything was there except the nerve of the butcher.

She drove down to Iva's store, then up the road again to the Smiths', and issued her invitations. Back home, she swept and scrubbed by fluorescent lantern light. She was surprised at her own excitement.

Earlier than usual she was up in the morning, hauling the endless buckets of water from the creek, filling the rabbits' water crocks and pellet feeders, checking the newborns, putting two does in with bucks for breeding while she cleaned the droppings trays.

She breakfasted on eggs spiced with green peppers and onions from the garden, bread toasted on a fork over the stove's burner hole, tea, and half a cantaloupe. The other half rested in the food safe in the spring. The safe was full now, with lettuce, eggs, tomatoes, and the ever-producing green beans.

"Okay. This is it." She spoke firmly to herself via Urchin. Leaving her breakfast dishes soaking in a bucket on the back of the stove, she took herself mentally by the scruff of the neck and walked herself to the barn.

To the first doomed doe Jane said, "I'm sorry, but it has

to be done. I'm sorry." She opened the cage door, picked up the doe by the loose flesh over her shoulders, and brought her out. The doe struggled in her grasp. Red knowing eyes stared into Jane's.

"Don't look at me like that."

She took a few hard breaths to steady herself, then pulled in a long breath and held it. She suspended the doe by her hind legs, straddled the narrow neck with her fingers and gave a sharp jerk downward and back, as the rabbit books said. The doe fought and cried but didn't die.

"Come on," Jane muttered grimly. Again she jerked and this time there was an internal crack, and the doe hung still.

A ringing began in Jane's ears; her legs went rubbery.

"Hang on, you're doing fine," she said in a loud, odd-sounding voice. She made her feet carry her outdoors into the sunshine, the dead doe still in her hand. Deep breathing helped. She shook her head and continued around the corner of the barn. Focus on the job at hand, she thought. With shaky fingers she tightened the nailed-up wire loops around the two hind feet, suspending the doe, belly-out, against the rough weather-grayed planks of the barn wall.

Following the memorized instructions in her books, she slit the doe's hide from heel to heel, cut off the forelegs and slowly pulled the skin downward and off. It was surprisingly easy. She almost managed a laugh. With the lightness of relief she worked the hide onto a loop of wire that she thought her father had used for this purpose. It acted as a sweater stretcher, to keep the hide from shrinking while it dried. She hung it on a nail out of the way, to deal with later.

Jane took another break to walk in an aimless circle, breathing deeply and looking at bloodless treetops. When she came back to the carcass, it was just that, no longer a doe but a form, meat and bones, edible groceries. With a feeling of growing power she laid it on the stump and hacked it into drumsticks and four large body chunks, and dropped it into a bucket of cold water.

"Yay-hoo!"

With the second doe Jane managed the kill in one swift, hard motion. It brought moments of queasiness and a little ear-ringing, but much less than the first. This carcass she left whole, for roasting.

The third doe was dispatched with something very near confidence.

"I did it," Jane yelled. There was glory in her voice as she said again, more quietly, "I did it."

"Did what?" A man's voice came from around the corner of the barn. Aaron Bruns appeared, grinning.

"What are you doing here?" Startled, she sounded less glad than she was.

He looked polished and spiffy in white shorts, green polo shirt, and unmarred running shoes. His legs were tanned, and the sun glinted in his curls and radiated from his face.

"That's a fine welcome after I drove all the way down here just to see you. I believe I'll pass on the handshake though, if you don't mind. What have you been doing, murder?"

Pain flashed through Jane, but he didn't notice. Of course, she reminded herself, Aaron didn't know about her parents.

"Just a little home butchering," she said. This time her

voice had its normal rich timbre. "I wasn't expecting company, that's all. I mean, I'm expecting company for dinner, I just wasn't expecting you. What are you doing down this way on a Sunday?"

She began sidestepping toward the creek. As he talked she kicked off her shoes and waded into the water, soap in hand, and washed the blood off her arms and face. The red-spattered jeans and T-shirt would have to wait. Uneasily she tried to remember whether she'd combed her hair yet that morning. Sometimes she forgot for an entire day, knowing no one would see her.

"Just riding around. Thought I'd look you up, see what your place was like. Woman at the gas station down the road told me where you lived."

Awkwardly Jane stood erect in the shallow water and said, "I'm glad you came. I'm going to try roasting a couple of old rabbits for dinner, for my neighbors. Can you stay for dinner?"

He stayed. "But you don't want to roast indoors on a hot day like this," he said. "I'll rig you up a spit out in the yard, okay? We can cook those rascals over a wood fire. Guaranteed to make even tough old rabbits delicious."

While Jane changed into clean clothes and put potatoes in the oven to bake and began snapping and stringing the beans, Aaron worked outside. He made a fire-holding ring of rocks on the ground, drove two forked sticks into the earth on either side, and rummaged in the barn till he found an iron rod the right size, which he scrubbed in the creek.

Coming back to the house he detoured to the edge of the

woods for fistfuls of wild pink daisies and some smaller blue-purple flowers, which Jane arranged in a water glass in the center of the table.

By the time the Smiths and Iva drove in, almost together, the rabbit carcasses were browning and dripping savory juices onto the fire. Beans and onions simmered on the stove, and a scrubbed water bucket held a salad of garden lettuce, tomato chunks, carrots, and peppers.

With his natural good humor Aaron fitted in easily with the others. The meat proved a little tough and tasteless within its wood-smoked crust, but no one cared.

Jane sat at the head of her rickety table listening to the banter of her friends, looking at the food she had created, and she was infused with a soul-deep satisfaction.

SEVEN

Several days later Jane butchered two young fryer-sized rabbits, wrapped the meat in plastic wrap, stretched the hides on drying frames, and got into the jeep. At Iva's store she parked in front of the gas pump and took the meat inside.

"Would you trade me some fresh young rabbit for a tank of gas?"

"Love to." Iva took the meat and dropped it into the freezer.

"I'm not supposed to sell it because of Federal regulations," Jane said, "but I don't know why we couldn't do a little trading now and then, if that would be okay with you."

They worked out a compromise between the two dollars apiece Freez-Fine would have paid for the rabbits and the eight dollars Iva would have had to pay for them in the grocery store. Five dollars' worth of gas, groceries, or cash for each rabbit. Jane took five in gas and five in cash and headed for Prosper.

Beside her on the seat lay a flat package wrapped in grocery-bag paper. It contained the three hides from Sunday's roaster rabbits, on their way to a tanner in Excelsior Springs who advertised on the bulletin board in the laundromat. For fifty cents apiece he would tan the hides, turning the stiff skin into pliable leather.

Buyers awaited the hides when they came back tanned. Another of Marian's church friends, whose consuming hobby was making fancy character dolls and selling them at craft fairs, wanted as many hides as Jane could sell her, to make hats, muffs, and jackets for her ice-skater dolls. Another woman in the church's sewing circle was interested in learning to sew the hides together to make a jacket for her granddaughter. Five dollars per hide, Jane had told them, and they eagerly agreed.

During the hour that it took the jeep to bounce and sway the thirty-five hilly, twisted miles from home to Fayetteville, Jane thought about the shopping she planned to do. Smiling, she told herself, "I really am getting weird. Buying my own birthday presents, for heaven's sake . . . well, it's not that weird when you think about it. It's kind of logical. I need somebody to do nice things for, and I need somebody to do nice things for me. If I don't happen to have anyone like that in my life right now, why not be both giver and receiver for myself? I think it's logical."

Her first stop was at the pet shop, where she delivered four bunnies. The shop was in a mall. Ordinarily Jane closed her eyes to the dress shops, shoe shops, and bath

shops around her and hurried away with her money intact.
Today she lingered.

She had intended to buy warm socks for the coming
winter and maybe a new hooded sweatshirt, but after coast-
ing through every store in the mall, after losing the mental
battle against the hope that Aaron would come to the clearing again, in the end she bought a small bottle of Charlie
cologne and a lace blouse marked down to half price.

"Gift wrap them, please," she said.

In the bakery at the end of the mall she bought the small-
est birthday cake they had. With candles.

Virtuously she waited the two days until August six-
teenth before she unwrapped the presents and ate the cake.
Her other gift to herself was a day off, except for the necessary chores of caring for the animals and cooking her
meals. For the rest of the time she lay on her bed wearing
the lace blouse above her shorts, sniffing her Charlie-
scented wrists, and reading romance novels.

It was easily the best birthday she'd ever had.

The next day, when she took a cageful of rabbits to the
Freez-Fine truck, Aaron said, "I'm going down to Fort
Smith Sunday to a rabbit show, just for the heck of it. Want
to come along? It's kind of fun to see all the different
breeds."

Behind her shy smile Jane was so elated she almost forgot her check for the sixteen rabbits.

Her excitement woke her on Sunday while the sky was still
dark. She lay in bed as long as she could bear to, telling
herself this was her first real date, telling herself not to go

off half-cocked, it wasn't a real date. Telling herself yes, it was, too. He'd asked her, he was coming to pick her up, they were spending the day together because he wanted her company. If that wasn't a date, what was?

To make it even more perfect, the day would be spent doing the one thing she wanted most to do, seeing every kind of rabbit she'd read about: Angoras and Lops and Siamese and Chinchilla, and New Zealand Whites like her own, for comparison. Today was the day.

But it was Aaron, not the rabbit show, that put helium in her stride as she moved through the morning chore routine. It was for Aaron that she bathed in the cold creek water, in a blanket of morning fog so thickly white she could hardly see the water. It was for Aaron she gritted her teeth and lowered her scalp into the icy water for a shampoo, then ran with blue lips and fingernails back to the house to jab up the fire in the stove.

She dressed in her best, white-duck jeans and a red cotton Wal-Mart top, wishing for a fleeting instant that they were going somewhere appropriate for the lace blouse. Maybe our next date, she told herself with uncharacteristic optimism.

She ate a nervous-stomach breakfast of tea and bread with jam, sitting with her back close to the stove to dry her hair. She decided not to risk lipstick for fear of drawing attention to her ugly mouth, but at the last minute she rubbed some Charlie onto her wrists.

He picked her up at eight, smiling, joking, full of himself. The two-hour drive to Fort Smith was filled almost entirely by Aaron's conversation—about Aaron, but he did it in such an amusing way that it didn't seem egotistical, just entertaining. On the rare occasions when Jane offered a thought, he listened and commented, although he never asked her questions.

She told him briefly that her parents were dead and she'd been raised by an aunt and uncle in Rogers whom she never saw anymore. That seemed to satisfy his curiosity about her.

They found the rabbit show in a National Guard armory building at the edge of town. It was a tan glazed-brick building surrounded by trim lawns and a large parking lot, filled that morning with station wagons, vans, and pickups from all over the Midwest. Walking through the lot toward the building, Jane spotted license plates from Texas, Minnesota, even Georgia.

Inside, the building was one huge room filled with rows of tables of rabbit cages, milling people, and, at one end, an area of judging tables. With Aaron's fingertips steering her back, Jane moved slowly down rows of cages, looking past the owners to see the rabbits within.

Owners sat on folding chairs before their cages, talking with each other, eating doughnuts and drinking coffee from paper cups, shouting jokes toward distant friends, or quietly reading judging schedules. Most met Jane's glance with ready smiles.

But it was the rabbits that drew Jane's attention and held it. They were huge, dazzling-clean animals, glowing with care and health and quality. The New Zealand Whites looked much as Jane's pedigreed animals would have looked, groomed as these were. She glowed in the assurance that at least some of hers were good enough to have been here.

She came across the breeder from whom she had ordered her stock, introduced herself to him, told him yes, she was very pleased with her rabbits, they were doing well, their first offspring were going into the breeding herd now.

The man opened one of the cages behind him and drew out a mammoth buck, setting him on a small grooming table that jutted into the aisle. "This old boy is the sire of your buck," the man said. "This one was grand show champion at Harrison the last two years, and he's got a good shot at breed champion, at least, here today. You ought to get that buck of yours entered in a few shows. You can get a lot more for your breeding stock with a champion or two in the pedigree. How much you selling your breeding stock for?"

"I haven't sold any for breeding," Jane admitted. "Just for meat, and just the ones from the other herd. The good ones I'm keeping for myself."

The man nodded. "Well, you get a few of those young ones out to some shows, and you'll be able to get twenty-five, thirty dollars apiece for them like I'm doing. They're good enough. You join ARBA if you haven't already, and they'll send you show information."

Jane agreed and moved on, thinking, *Twenty-five dollars apiece. A hundred breeding does times five litters a year. . . .*

Aaron had stopped to talk to someone so Jane moved on to the rows of fancy breeds. The luxuriously shaggy Angoras caught her heart. The mournful French Lops, with their ears splayed out like hound puppies' on the cage floors, made her grin and tilt her head. What appeal they would have in pet shops, she thought. Much more than the ordinary white bunnies. Worth much more, too. . . .

A sharp-faced young woman with a picture of a French Lop on her shirt front and two small children whining around her legs smiled at Jane.

"Are these yours?" Jane nodded toward the cages.

"These three here," the woman said. "Do you have Lops?"

"I've never seen any before, but I love their expressions. I've just got New Zealand Whites. But I was thinking about expanding into maybe either Angoras or Lops. I was thinking they might be good sellers in pet shops."

The woman looked offended. "Well, you'd never catch any of my stock in a pet shop."

"Why not?"

"They're too valuable. Pet shops don't pay anything like what they're worth, and besides, most pet buyers don't take all that good care of young rabbits. I sell only to other hobby breeders, for showing."

Jane digested this. "How much do you sell yours for?"

"Seventy-five for a show-quality buck, sixty to seventy for does."

The woman pulled a business card out of a hip pocket, swatted a child's finger away from his nose, and handed the card to Jane. "If you're interested, let me know. I usually have a waiting list for my young show stock, but I've got a few extra right now. Be glad to ship you a pair."

Aaron appeared with hot dogs and Cokes in a cardboard tray above his head, and they made their way to rows of folding chairs at one of the judging tables. While they ate, they watched the judging of a class of three-to-six-month-old tans, a process that was dramatic only to the owners of the animals involved. The two judges examined each rabbit, compared score sheets, and fastened ribbons to cages. The cages were removed and a new batch brought in. Next class.

"This is about as exciting as watching cars rust," Aaron whispered. "Let's take off, should we?"

Jane wanted to stay and watch the New Zealand White judging. She felt a need to know more about what the judges were looking for, so she'd know which of her young stock to enter in shows. She wanted to watch the French Lops and the Angoras, to learn what she could about them. She wanted to talk to more breeders, to compare prices and find out what faults or problems to beware of if she bought into a new breed.

The thought passed fleetingly through her head that she wished she'd come alone, so she could stay till she was ready to leave.

But that was crazy. She shook her head. When someone who looked like Aaron asked out someone who looked like her, it was crazy to wish it away. Shrugging, she said, "I'm ready to go anytime you are."

On their way out of town they passed an antique car show and flea market and spent the rest of the afternoon there. Jane tagged along while Aaron stroked chrome and talked to car owners and revved up an olive-green-and-black Model A station wagon with real wood sides, at the invitation of its owner.

Supper was sliced-beef sandwiches at an Arby's. They finished the fries and Cokes on the drive north toward home. Again the conversation centered around Aaron. Jane sat back and let him talk on. Her mind was on the Cahill Rabbitry, converted to fancy show stock, French Lops at seventy-five dollars apiece, maybe some Angoras for the pleasure of looking at them and burying her hands in their long wool.

It makes sense, she told herself. *It costs as much to raise a two-dollar rabbit for Freez-Fine as it costs to raise a seventy-five dollar fancy show animal. With my limited space I'd never be able to earn more than just starvation wages selling meat rabbits. But with expensive ones, the same barn space and the same feed bills could give me a genuinely comfortable life. Of course there would be show expenses, advertising in breeder magazines, and only maybe half of the young would actually get sold at show prices, but still. . . .*

It was an exciting possibility, a new turn to her dreams for herself and her future.

"Don't you think so?" Aaron asked.

"Yes. What?"

"I said, I don't think it would be worth sacrificing the credits I've already got in math to change my minor at this late date, don't you agree?"

"Oh. Absolutely."

He shot her a crooked grin, as though he knew she'd dropped out of the conversation but didn't especially care.

It was almost dark when they drove into the clearing.

70

Jane rushed through the evening feeding and checking, then washed up and settled on the purple sofa in the kitchen, beside Aaron. Wordlessly he pulled her to him and kissed her.

She didn't know what to say, so she said nothing, just looked at him, trying to read in his face what the kiss had meant to him. He was smiling, teasing.

For nothing in the world would she have admitted to him that it was her first kiss. Eighteen. Ridiculous. *By eighteen most girls aren't even virgins anymore,* she thought. But then, most girls had more opportunities than she'd had. *It's easy to stay on the straight and narrow when you're built that way,* she kidded herself.

Then there was no more time for thought. Aaron pulled her close again, and this time he left no doubt that he intended the kiss as the first step toward the bed.

He moved his head toward the bedroom and whispered, "Shall we get comfortable?"

"No."

She sat up away from him and frowned thoughtfully into his eyes.

"Am I moving too fast for you?" His voice was casual.

"You sure are."

"Okay. No big deal." He wrapped an arm around her and pulled her close and they sat back, her head in the hollow of his neck. He said, "Boy, I'd love to get my hands on something like that Model T wagon this afternoon. Wasn't that a classic, though?"

"Aaron," she said quizzically, pushing away to look at him.

71

"What, hon?"

"Well, one minute you're trying to make love to me and the next you're talking about cars."

He laughed. "You said you didn't want to. Okay. No big deal. I don't have to go begging, you know."

"I'm sure you don't," she said stiffly. "In fact, I'm sure I'm well below your usual standard."

"Why do you say that?" It was his turn to look puzzled.

"Come on. You know. I'm not exactly Miss Universe."

"Oh, that isn't it," he said.

"What isn't what?"

He sat up away from her. "Well, if you want to know the truth, the thing that puts me off about you is that you're so . . . independent. I mean the way you live and all that. You give the impression that you don't need anyone for anything."

"That's not true. I do need people." But as she said it, she wondered.

His eyes gleamed. "Then if you need me, let's go in the bedroom."

She shook her head, smiling sadly. "No, if that's the price you charge for your company, I'm not about to pay it."

"Fair enough. It's your decision." He yawned and stretched and scratched his leg, and in a few minutes he left.

Lying in her bed that night with the windows open to night breeze and insect song, with Urchin stretched warmly against her leg, Jane replayed every minute, every word, of the date.

Out of the confusion of her thoughts about Aaron, one realization surfaced and refused to go away. Living alone was going to mean putting more than physical distance between herself and potential friends or lovers. Her choice of life-style was going to frighten away the men Iva had talked about, men who needed to be leaned upon. New people, meeting Jane, would assume that she neither needed nor wanted closeness, and they would keep their distance.

And it's not true, she cried silently. *I need to be loved, like anybody else. Just . . . not. . .*

She didn't know what she meant. But the ache Aaron had left warned her that buying her own birthday presents was not always going to be enough.

EIGHT

Aaron stayed in Jane's head, waking and sleeping, as the days of the next week started slowly past. There were no young fryers ready to market that week, so she was pretty sure she wouldn't see Aaron again until Sunday.

Although he had said nothing about seeing her again when he drove away after the rabbit show, Jane knew he'd come again next Sunday. With no phone at her house, he couldn't call to make the date, but Sunday was his only day off and he'd be back.

She filled the days as well as she could. One of the jeep's tires succumbed to the slicing rocks of her road. She spent a morning rolling it down the highway to Iva's station, facing the verdict that it was shot beyond hope, and buying a new retread to be paid for with her next four fryers. She rolled the newly shod wheel back up the hill, down her road, and onto the waiting jeep's lugs, grimly promising

74

herself that her next free money was going toward a spare tire. That night she dreamed that the wheel came off, for lack of proper tightening, as she was driving down a steep mountain road.

One of her does, a nervous young animal, kindled her first litter and promptly killed all the newborn babies by smashing them as she tore frantically in and out of the nest box.

One of the older Shaffley bucks went off his feed for two days, and when Jane tried to catch him to examine him, he bit her, driving his long, yellow teeth through the base of her thumbnail. She left him alone in a fury and the next morning he was dead in his cage. Not knowing what he'd died of, she skinned him but didn't eat him, throwing the carcass into the woods for the wild animals. Then she worried for three days about her thumb, about dying from rabies, about epidemics wiping out her herd. She watched the other rabbits constantly and saw her dreams tottering. But there were no more deaths. She replaced the buck with a young one from the pedigreed herd and gradually ceased to worry.

On Tuesday, with the help of Beau's woodworking tools and Marian's china-decorating paints, she made a rabbit-shaped plywood sign that said, "Cahill Rabbitry," and nailed it to a tree beside the highway.

On Thursday a young couple drove in and asked to see the rabbits. They had bought a few from a Mr. Shaffley down by Mountaintop, they said, and were interested in upgrading their quality now. When Jane showed them the differences between her Shaffley stock and the pedigreed herd, they bought three pedigreed bucks and two does, twenty dollars apiece.

That night Jane wrote to the woman she'd talked to at the rabbit show and ordered a pair of French Lops. The spare tire for the jeep could wait a little longer, she decided. It was more important to get her start in a more valuable breed so that, a few years down the road, she could afford new tires instead of retreads.

On Friday it rained, a low-ceilinged, gray, drizzling rain that promised to go on and on. Jane lingered over the rabbit chores, enjoying the coziness of the barn and the company of her placid-faced bunnies. Eventually, hungry for breakfast, she ran back to the house, Urchin leaping and complaining at her side.

For the first time in weeks, the fire from the wood stove felt good. After she'd eaten, Jane sat for a long time at the wobbly wooden table drinking tea and staring out through streaming windowpanes.

A daydream began playing through her head. It had been forming all week, but she'd held it off with work projects.

She was a housewife, sitting here in this kitchen but not alone. Her husband Aaron sat across from her, looking at her with love in his eyes. He got up and kissed her good-bye and drove off to his teaching job in Prosper, and she spent the day cleaning the house. There was a long new addition to the house across the back, bathroom behind kitchen, bedroom behind present bedroom, now living room. The kitchen was a real one, with plumbing and a refrigerator, and somewhere a gas furnace . . . electric lights and a television set; and the rabbits in the barn were her hobby only. Weekend family trips to rabbit shows. And the children. . . .

No.

She cupped her chin in her hand and thought about children. Women were supposed to long for children. Did she? Jane probed the prospect and found it disturbing.

The good part of having children, she thought, *would be having someone who automatically loved you and needed you. You would be the most important person in that child's life, for a few years anyway, and that would feel wonderful.*

But.

She sidled around the edges of the admission. She honestly didn't want to be that continuously *with* another human being. Years and years of being always tuned to another person, checking constantly to be sure he was safe, setting aside her own thoughts and needs to take care of someone else's.

But if it's your own child, half you and half the man you love, it won't seem that way, she told herself. *You'll want to be with the baby, the toddler, the child. It will be a pleasure.*

She frowned, unconvinced.

Without asking herself why, she got up and climbed slowly up the ladder to the attic loft. She hoisted herself through the floor hole and sat there, legs dangling into the kitchen below, eyes moving slowly around the shadowy attic.

It was lit, dimly on this dark morning, by two small windows at the gable ends of the house. The attic was as long as kitchen and bedroom combined but only half as wide because of the slope of the roof. One end, over the bed-room, was bare except for a few cardboard boxes of her parents' belongings. The other end, over the kitchen, was furnished with a child-sized maple bed, braided rag rugs so dusty they showed no color at all, and a flat-topped wooden chest under the window. A hand-hewn wooden rod nailed to the roof supports held three child's dresses on rusty wire hangers. A square hole in the floor, covered with a black iron grill, admitted heat from the wood stove di-rectly below it.

Jane got up and wandered over to the grill and stood on it as she had when she was tiny Janey, catching heat in her flannel nightgown and watching it billow out like an old-fashioned lady's hoopskirt.

She sat on the bed and felt the prickle of the straw mat-tress. Only twice in these eight months had she come up-stairs, once with Beau to replace broken windowpanes and check the stovepipe, again later to search the boxes for anything usable. Both times she'd avoided this end of the attic.

Now, for the first time in her life, she tried to put herself into her mother's mind. She imagined herself Evangeline Cahill, with a tiny daughter Janey and a husband whom she and the baby had to fear.

She wondered how often, how passionately, Evangeline must have longed to be unmarried again. She must have sat on this bed looking down at her sleeping daughter and wondered if the daughter were worth the marriage.

Why had she married Ed Cahill? Was she lonely? Did she feel the way Jane had felt last Sunday after Aaron left, aching with her need to feel warmth from another human being? Was she afraid of living and dying alone, of being an old maid in the eyes of the community? Did she love him?

Had Evangeline felt that being tied to another human being day and night for twenty years was too much, the twenty years it took for a child to grow and depart? Had she been dismayed by her daughter's birth or was it a blessing, in her uncherished life, to have this girl child to hug and rock and talk to?

Jane pondered. Maybe—no, probably Evangeline had sat looking down at her sleeping daughter and feared that the father's savagery was alive in the child. Vague memories began to wake in Jane, of lying in this bed, her mother's worried face above her, a hand tenderly brushing the hair away from her forehead, drawing a line down her nose ending with a beep of the nose to make Janey giggle.

She turned and sat cross-legged in the center of the low bed, hugging her knees and staring into middle space.

If she were married to Aaron, and if they had a little girl, and if Aaron came in from the barn carrying a bloodied skinning knife and towered over the child. . .

She grew suddenly cold and rigid. Memory rose from rambling thought: not Aaron. Pa. It was Pa standing over her with the skinning knife and bellowing, "Doyle's bastard," meaningless but terrifying words.

And the next morning, the explosion, and Evangeline looking calmly over the rim of the floor hole and saying, "Get dressed...we're going to town...not with Pa."

Shivering, Jane got up and went back down the ladder into the kitchen. She put the saucepan of tea water back on the stove's burner hole and went to stand in the doorway of the bedroom.

Doyle's bastard. Could that be true? Could Evangeline of the worried face and stroking hand have been unfaithful to her monster husband, with his own brother, and produced a child whose presence drove him to the destructive rages that were Jane's only real memory of him?

She stared thoughtfully at the bed that was now her own, her comfort place for afternoon reading and night burrowing with the purring cat. Was that bed a place of torment for her mother? For her father? Strange thought. Had there been love between them once?

Had Evangeline clung to the far edge of the bed and slept in uncomfortable tension for years of nights?

Twelve years now, since it had happened. . . . Twelve years of carefully not thinking about it, about them. No memory of her father, since none was bearable . . . only occasional thoughts of her mother because of Evangeline's clearly stated wish after her sentencing: No letters from Janey. No visits from Doyle or Marlyce. Let the child forget her existence. And one last apology for lacking the courage for suicide.

Jane had been all too willing. Although her five-year-old mind had an unclear grasp of homicide and prison sentences, she understood with painful clarity that her mother had done something so terrible that Janey herself was shunned by good people. It was easier to close her mind to her mother, to memories of her father, even to memories of home in the clearing.

Easier to concentrate on the fearful challenge of the big

town school, the kindergarten room filled with more children than she'd ever seen at one time. Then came first grade and the new escape into storybooks. More years, more grades, more effective escapes from the people around her; bicycle escapes into the country around Rogers, longer and deeper escapes into books.

Now, she thought, the biggest escape of all, ironically full circle to the house and the life here, but blessedly alone.

What am I doing to myself? Am I cutting myself off from love and marriage and motherhood just out of cowardice?

It wouldn't be the same for me as it was for Ma. I wouldn't marry somebody like him. But then, Pa probably didn't seem that way to her, before she married him.

Past past past past past. *Get out of it,* she told herself angrily. *Get back into the real world.*

But there was something she needed to do first. She ran through the rain to the barn and brought back, under her shirt, the dime-store notebook in which she kept her records of breeding and expenses. She turned to a clean page at the back, sat down at the table, and began.

Dear Mother,

I feel funny writing to you after all these years, but I wanted to make contact. I hope it's all right with you. I'm living back in our house now, and it's made me think about you, and what happened.

First, my news. I graduated from high school last January and moved back here the next day. I've been making my living raising rabbits. I just started it because the cages were here and it seemed logical, but by now I really love it, and I'm very happy. I'm selling an average of $100 a month worth of fryers to Freez-Fine, plus trading some to friends for gas for the jeep, and other stuff. I also trade rabbit meat to my neighbors for beef sometimes because they buy quarters of beef from some people at their church.

I'm also beginning to sell some of my pedigreed rabbits to other breeders, for herd improvement, and I'm going to be getting into French Lops and possibly Angoras, for showing, because you can sell them for quite a bit more than meat rabbits.

The house is still in pretty good shape. I've been working on fixing it up in my spare time. And I figured out how to tie up the springs in the sofa so it doesn't sag.

I put in a big garden, too. It's not as good as Aunt Marlyce's was because the soil isn't built up very well yet. Like my neighbor says, the best crop in an Arkansas garden is rocks. But I keep adding the rabbit manure and clearing out the rocks as they come up, so it should get better every year. Even as it is, I've been eating out of it steadily since May and canning lots, especially green beans.

Well, I didn't really write just to tell you about my vegetables. I wanted to know how you are. And also I wanted you to know how I am. I've turned out okay, I think. I'm kind of homely, but I'm getting so I don't mind that as much as I used to, living in town.

One thing I thought you might be worried about. I didn't turn out like Pa at all. I have finally learned to kill and dress the rabbits when I have to, but it was really hard at first and I still hate doing it. I have a very even temper, and I think the people around here who know me like me.

If you remember Iva Oliphant, who runs the little store and gas station south of here, she's getting to be a good friend of mine, also the Smiths, who live next door. They built their house after we moved away so you wouldn't know them, but they are very nice retired people from Kirksville. They always invite me on their family picnics when their kids and grandkids come to visit, so they must not think there's anything terrible about me being a Cahill.

I even have a boyfriend. His name is Aaron Bruns. He's in college at Cape Girardeau. He works the Freez-Fine route in the summer, which is how I met him. Last Sunday he took me to a rabbit show in Fort Smith, although we ended up spending most of the day looking at antique cars. He is very cute and nice, and he seems interested in me for some reason. Next time he comes I'll see if he has any pictures of himself that I could have, and if so I'll send you one.

If you would like to write to me, I would like to hear from you. I think twelve years is too long, don't you?

Your daughter, Jane.

It rained again on Saturday. Jane spent the day in the house, cleaning more thoroughly than usual. She scrubbed the linoleum floors and made dashes into the woods for wild flowers to arrange on the table and on the dresser in the bedroom. She didn't ask herself why she was decorating the bedroom.

In the afternoon she set the mirror by the kitchen sink at a light-catching angle and began cutting her hair. She lifted one strand at a time and cut by sliding the scissors down the strand as she cut. She was practiced at cutting her own hair by now, having started when she was nine because no one else was doing anything about it.

Although she had to do the back part by feel, by measuring with her finger and cutting blind, the end result was good. The tan waves arranged themselves in a soft cap that eased the angles of her face. She raked up the cut-off hair and threw it away with a feeling of satisfaction.

As on the previous Sunday, she was up at dawn the next day, hurrying through the chores. By seven the sun was up and the clearing was steamy warm. She bathed in the creek, washed her hair, and ran naked into the house to dress.

Shorts this time. *Casual,* she reminded herself. *Don't look as though you dressed for him, or were even expecting him.* Denim shorts, but clean, unholey ones; white cotton blouse. No makeup, no Charlie, but shining hair carefully arranged in the mirror over the sink.

Eight o'clock. Breakfast, breakfast dishes. It was an hour's drive from Rogers at the speed Aaron drove. It would be midmorning anyway before she could seriously begin to watch for him.

She sat on the porch step and tickled Urchin with a stem of foxtail. The sun grew hot. She moved to the shade, so she wouldn't be sweaty when he arrived.

84

At nine-thirty a car hummed in the woods, then appeared. Jane jumped up and started for the cabin, so he wouldn't catch her sitting on the steps waiting for him. But the car was gray, not Aaron's red Omni. Her hope curdled. The man in the car leaned his head through the window and asked if she sold dressed rabbit meat.

"I can't, I'm not government-inspected, but I can sell you live rabbits ready to butcher."

The man shook his head, his wife beside him shook her head, and they drove away.

But the one car seemed to make a second car more possible, and the next one would be his. Jane decided she'd greet him with a kiss when he got out of the car. They were going together, sort of. No harm in acting like it. Better to let him know she wasn't all that self-reliant. He'd be heading back to school in another week or so, not much time left. Only today and maybe another Sunday to cement things between them so that when he got back among all those girls on campus. . .

She didn't want to think about that.

At ten she got up and went inside, thinking that a picnic lunch would be good. If he wanted to go someplace, like the antique car show last week, they'd have her good homemade sandwiches to take along. Or if he wanted to stay home, they could just go over to the other side of the clearing where the lone butternut tree stood within the perimeter of the clearing, near the creek and within sound of the spring, a perfect place to picnic even if it was her front yard.

She cut thin slices of cold rabbit haunch and layered

them with Bibb lettuce from the garden and tomato slices and green disks of Marian's homemade dill pickles. She wrapped the sandwiches in the plastic she had used to package Iva's meat, then wandered back outside again.

At one o'clock she gave in to her hunger and ate a sandwich, knowing that Aaron would already have eaten by the time he came.

She then tried to read to pass the time, but her eyes unfocused and wandered from the page. She didn't want the time to pass. She wanted it to stop and wait for Aaron to come, so they could at least have the afternoon together.

By three she began admitting that he might not come after all. He never said he would, she reminded herself.

But with so few Sundays, probably only one more, before the end of his vacation, surely he wouldn't waste this one.

At five she gave up and did her evening chores without caution for the clean white blouse, and for supper she ate Aaron's picnic sandwiches.

She went to bed early and allowed herself a brief, throat-aching cry before her common sense began fighting to the surface.

After all, he hadn't said he was coming.

She held Urchin in her arms and stared at the flowers on the dresser and told herself she was all right. She didn't need him.

NINE

There were a dozen young rabbits approaching market size in the lower tier of cages. Every day the next week Jane took out two or three of them and weighed them. Not quite big enough. Churning with frustration she set them back in their cages and willed them to hurry and grow.

"Of course I could drop in on the Freez-Fine truck anyway," she told Urchin. "Just out of friendliness. I don't actually have to have anything to sell. Aaron's a friend of mine. It's logical that I'd be casually curious to know when he's going back to school."

Urchin cocked her head and looked wise.

"Oh. You think he'd see through that and think I was chasing him."

The cat yawned, flattening her whiskers and curling her sharp pink tongue.

"You're probably right. Better to play it cool."

She began walking the mile and a half out to the mailbox every day after lunch. Before this, mail had never been important enough for special trips. It was mostly catalogs full of things she couldn't afford, offers of prizes she'd never win, or pleas for charity she couldn't give. The jeep's tires were too thin and too precious for unnecessary scrambles over the sharp rocks of the road, so Jane walked.

Each day she pulled open the mailbox door telling herself not to hope for anything from him. She sorted through the junk mail, searching carefully through pages of catalogs, then walked dispiritedly back home again.

At the end of that long week came Labor Day weekend. She stayed clean and close to the house Saturday and Sunday but with a sinking certainty that he wasn't coming.

"He's probably back in Cape Girardeau by now. His school's starting. But why didn't he come by before he left? He wouldn't just go off and not even say good-bye. Something must have come up at the last minute, a family complication or something. He'll write to me and explain."

On Labor Day she told herself she'd wasted enough time waiting for Aaron to show up, and instead of staying at home listening for his car, she went with the Smiths and their family up to the Shepherd of the Hills tourist area in Southern Missouri.

She made the trip sitting on the floor of the son's conversion van with the three grandchildren, and with every mile they traveled, Jane grew looser and younger until she was on a level with the children. They were all in a silly mood, and they carried her with them.

It's never too late to have a happy childhood, she teased herself silently.

"Let's make up poems," the oldest boy said. "I'll start, and everybody take turns adding a line. Okay, here goes. There once was a man named Jeremiah. Your turn, Jane."

"Jeremiah." She made a face at him. "Okay, let's see. There once was a man named Jeremiah, who set his poor mother on fiah."

The van rang with laughter. Fleetingly it occurred to Jane that she had made a casual joke about family violence and neither she nor anyone else had cringed away from it. *I'm getting better,* she thought, elated.

Beau took up the poetry. "There once was a man named Jeremiah, who set his poor mother on fiah. When asked why he'd fried her—"

Marian chimed in. "He sat down beside her—"

Their daughter-in-law yelled from the back of the van, "And said, 'She always wanted to be a red-hot mama.'"

"That doesn't even rhyme," the children whooped, pelting her with pillow and empty potato chip bag.

At the Shepherd of the Hills Country, they followed a tour group through the cluster of log cabins on display and listened to the guide tell the stories behind the stories written there. Jane and the children rode rental horses through steep and densely wooded mountain trails while the adults browsed the gift shops.

After lunch in the resort's rustic restaurant, they all took seats on hewn logs set on the mountain slope and watched a wildly dramatic production of the Shepherd of the Hills story, complete with horses galloping out of the woods onto the stage area and the burning down of a log cabin, which was rebuilt each day for the next day's play. During a square dance scene, the actors came into the audience and pulled spectators into the dance, laughing and protesting and loving it. Jane silently wished to be chosen and wasn't, but it didn't dampen her enjoyment of the day.

That night, lying in her bed with Urchin across her ankle, she wondered if Aaron had come while she was away. She hoped so. She wanted him to know that she'd been out with friends having a wonderful time, independent of him.

"So how's your love life?" Iva asked lazily. She and Jane were seated at opposite ends of a battered green rowboat left over from the days when Iva's husband was failing at being a fisherman. The boat bobbed against its anchor in three feet of sparkling-clear river water, under an over-hanging butternut tree. The river had undercut the bank beneath the tree, so that its roots hung exposed and dying.

They were just a few miles upstream from Iva's store, at a spot where the river lay between high, rocky bluffs. The rocks showed rust-red through the deep greens of pin oak and cedar. The women had been there less than an hour and already the creel hanging over the side of the boat held half a dozen sizable catfish.

Jane smiled wryly. "I think the big one got away."

"That college boy I met at your place that time?"

Jane nodded.

"You never said nothing about him all this time. I didn't realize you had a thing going with him. What'd he do, go back to school?"

"I guess. I haven't heard from him. It wasn't any big romance, really. We just went out a couple of times."

There was a note in her voice that she hadn't intended.

Iva looked at her keenly from beneath the green plastic visor that shaded her eyes. "You're better off not getting involved with that one anyhow, girl. Count your blessings."

Jane bristled slightly. "Why do you say that? He's a nice guy."

Iva snorted. "I'm not saying he isn't. If you want to spend your life being his audience while he talks about himself. All I'm saying is, if you go hanging your heart on somebody like that, you're cruising for a bruising."

"I know," Jane said softly. "I'm not exactly up to his standards in the looks department, or the brains department either. Here I am, this weird old homely rabbit-skinner, hardly the type for him."

Iva pulled up her line and cast with whiplash emphasis. "Oh, come on. Do you really believe that stuff?"

"Don't you?"

"Not for a minute, and I don't think you do either. You're just in the habit of putting yourself down, and it's time you knocked it off."

"I'm not pretty," Jane said flatly.

"So what? Neither am I, and I think I'm the greatest thing since peanut butter. Neither was Eleanor Roosevelt or any number of other women who never let it get them down. You put your own value on yourself, girl. We all do."

"I know all that." Jane did know it, and she recognized with a start that when she'd said, just now, that she wasn't pretty, she was speaking from old habit, not from genuine feeling. There had been a gradual change recently in the way she looked at herself in the kitchen mirror when she combed her hair in the morning. The face she saw was that of her best friend, her own increasingly loved self. Now that she was no longer comparing it with the faces of the girls around her at school, she'd ceased to see it as crooked teeth and receding chin but saw it instead as a strong, familiar, good face.

Odd, she mused, smiling into the middle space upriver.

There was a tug and a splash on Iva's line. Another catfish surfaced and was pried off the hook and dropped into the creel with the others. Iva had offered freezer space for Jane's half of the catch, and Jane savored the prospect of catfish dinners this winter.

Her thoughts meandered back to the conversation. "It still kind of bothers me, how much I'm beginning to like living alone. I mean, the longer I do it the more spoiled to it I get. Pretty soon it's going to get so I never will want to get married."

"So don't get married. You can make yourself a very nice life right where you are, girl. You don't need anyone to do it for you."

"I know that. What bothers me is, it seems so selfish. Such a selfish way to live, just for yourself. I feel like everybody should be, you know, putting something back, some way."

"Reproducing yourself for the continuation of the race?"

"Yeah, something like that."

"Hon, that was a good belief back in the days when the human race was getting started. At this point it's in more danger from overpopulation than under. And there's different ways of making the world better. Just making the people around you a little happier for the moment, or feeding people with the rabbits you raise, or breeding a pet for some child to love, that's adding to the world."

"Well, yes, in a way, but I don't know. It still seems like a basically selfish way to live."

"Listen, girl, if you are taking care of yourself, not living off the government or being a drain on other people, that's the main thing. From that point on, anything you add is in the credit column. Heck, *I* like you. You're good company because you're interested in other people. You're kind and thoughtful, and you see the good side of people and situations. You don't need to worry about whether or not you're making a contribution to the world, living like you do. You're okay."

They fished silently for several minutes. Then Iva said, "There's a difference between selfish like you're talking about, and self . . . how can I say it? Self-contained, I guess. You like to do things for yourself and take care of yourself, and that's all to the good. *Selfish* is somebody that's always out for himself at other people's cost, like trying to screw the other guy in a deal, or trampling on people's feelings, or like that. See the difference? You're not like that at all."

"Hm." Jane pondered.

"What you are is self-contained."

Jane snorted. "That's what Aaron said. He said I intimidated him because I was so self-sufficient I didn't need anybody."

"Need." Iva shrugged. "Well, he's probably right in a way. People like you and me, we don't actually need—how

93

can I say this—we don't depend on other people for our happiness. Oh, friendship, sure. Some of that. But I mean, we don't have to go looking for someone outside ourselves to *provide* our happiness for us. We can manufacture it for ourselves. Then, when we find people we care about, we can give out of that supply that we've made for ourselves instead of hanging around their necks and whining and demanding that they marry us and take care of us and *make us happy*. See?"

"Mmm."

They fell silent again. Jane moved her line back and forth slowly through the water and absorbed Iva's words. Gradually she began to smile.

After that day, she quit making special trips to the mailbox.

September moved past with gradually cooling days and the first chilly nights. Goldenrod and yellow daisies gilded the clearing, and the south sides of the prickly ash and butternut trees faded toward tan. The air was vigorously dry, the afternoons sparkling with sun and energy.

On a pet-shop run to Fayetteville, Jane passed a garage sale and stopped, just to look. She'd sold her first French Lop bunnies, six of them for fifteen dollars apiece, so when she saw the small used chain saw amid the clutter of garden tools at the garage sale, she bought it in a hang-the-expense mood. Its price sticker said twenty-five dollars. She offered twenty and got it. With the other five, which she considered to be earned fun money, she bought two pictures and a box full of paperback books.

Beau came over the next day and showed her how to start the chain saw, easing the choke from open to half-open after the first two pulls so it didn't flood, and bracing her foot against the hand bar when she pulled the starter cord. He told her repeatedly how to handle it and fussed over the idea of her using it alone.

"Those things are dangerous, even if you're used to handling them. They can kick back and get you in the leg, or they can throw a chain and slice your hand all to hell. You better just use it when I can be with you."

Jane muttered a noncommittal answer but told herself that she couldn't be dependent on him, she'd have to learn to use it as safely as possible herself and take her chances.

She and Beau spent the afternoon in her woods, cutting down small, crowded trees, cutting dead limbs off old oaks and butternuts, and slicing off at ground level saplings and brambles that blocked the ghost of an old timber road.

Jane's land was a forty-acre square, with the clearing roughly in the middle. In her treks through the woods in search of handy fuel, she'd come upon three loops of timber roads circling out from the clearing and back to it. They were almost invisible except from certain angles, and then they showed up primarily as absence of large trees in ten-foot-wide paths. New growth was already head-high.

She decided to make a fall project out of clearing at least one of the loops so that she could drive it in the jeep. It would make firewood hauling infinitely easier than with the wheelbarrow.

For the next two weeks all her time between morning and evening rabbit chores was filled with woods work.

Sometimes Beau came over to help, but mostly she worked alone. The first time she jerked the chain saw into life, she was clammy with apprehension, imagining blood gushing from her ripped flesh. But, as with the butchering of the rabbits, the bad part was quickly behind her. Within a few days she was handling the saw with skill and care. Beau ceased to hold his breath when she fired it up.

By the end of the second week her loop of timber road was passable by jeep. She celebrated by inviting the Smiths and Iva for a catfish dinner. Accomplishment and companionship and buoyant self-satisfaction glowed within her.

The next day she checked the mailbox on her way to Prosper. There, between the Sears Fall Sale catalog and a contest offer from Publishers Clearing House, lay a personal letter. Her heart thudded as she turned over the envelope. But it wasn't from Cape Girardeau.

It was from the state women's reformatory.

Jane stared at it. In the month since she had written to her mother, she had almost ceased to expect an answer. That rainy August afternoon and her own letter had begun to seem distant and unreal, buried beneath her preoccupation with Aaron and the more immediate demands of her daily life.

Turning off the jeep's ignition and sitting back in her seat, she pulled out the letter and read it. It was written on plain typing paper, in handwriting that was like connected printing. *I don't even know my own mother's handwriting,* she thought numbly.

Dear Daughter,
I was surprised and glad to get your letter. I've been

trying to decide what to say to you. When I came here I said that I wanted you to forget about me and about what happened, but that was for your benefit, not mine.

As you can imagine, I've spent many hours thinking about you and wondering what kind of girl you were growing into. If you think you would like to write to me from time to time and tell me about your life, there is nothing that would make me happier. You are old enough by now to make that decision.

I was surprised to hear that you were living back in Prosper. I thought you would have sold the place, maybe for money for your education. I'm glad you didn't. As you may know, I was born in that house and spent a very happy childhood there. I was always so sorry that I couldn't have given you the same happy childhood. I would like to hear more about your rabbit business and your boyfriend, and especially about you. If you could send me a picture of yourself that would mean so much to me.

As for myself, I'm used to the life here. I don't have it too badly. I've been a trustee for seven years now, and I work in the library. I'm treated well, and I've made some good friends here.

I am afraid to ask this, which is why I put off answering your letter for so long, but I will ask it anyway. If you ever come over this way it would be the dream of my life to see you. We have open visiting hours on weekends.

Your loving mother.

TEN

Jane had expected bars and glass partitions and telephones to talk through. The visitors' room at the state women's reformatory was a pleasant surprise. It was a large room, painted seasick green but lightened by a wall of windows and groups of chairs and sofas.

She thought, *This is worse than butchering my first rabbit.* Back straight, feet straight and close together on the carpet, fingers tangled and twisting, she waited. She wore the only skirt she owned that still fit her and the white blouse in which she'd waited for Aaron.

It had already been a nerve-stretching day, just getting here. The jeep had blown a tire thirty miles from home, and since she hadn't yet bought the spare, she'd had to flag a ride for herself and the wheel, find a service station that was more than a self-serve convenience store, wait while the tire was patched, and find a ride back to the jeep.

Changing a tire is twice as hard, she learned, when you have to keep your blouse clean.

Finally moving again, she made another discovery. An open jeep with no top and low side doors might be fine for bouncing around in the woods, but in fast, busy, freeway traffic nearing the city, it left her feeling nervously exposed. Semis whooshed past, their wind flattening her clothes against her body and blowing her hair across her face.

Now, having found the reformatory and her way through the gates and doors and officialities, there was no time to unclench from the drive. Her mother was yet to be faced.

She expected not to recognize Evangeline. Her memory of that part of her life was clouded by time and the need to forget. She carried only hazy impressions of her mother's face in her mind. There had been no photographs.

But the woman who appeared across the visitors' room and stood scanning the room struck a chord in Jane and set her vibrating like piano wire. The woman was small, much smaller than Jane, with a face that reminded Jane of her rabbits. The features were finer than Jane's and more regular, but with the same receding chin and overcrowded mouth. On this small, round-shouldered person the face was sweet and defenseless and seemed to ask for protection.

Her eyes passed Jane, then returned and held. The woman didn't smile but moved toward Jane as a sleepwalker moves. She wore ordinary clothing, knit slacks and an overblouse, inexpensive things but not the gray, numbered uniforms Jane had expected.

Standing awkwardly, Jane looked down at Evangeline Cahill. *This is her,* played over and over in her mind. She could think of nothing to say.

"I was hoping you'd come," the woman said simply.

"Yes. I got your letter."

For a long moment they stood looking at each other. There was too much to say and no way to start it. Finally, Evangeline made a vague motion toward the sofa behind Jane, and together they sat. Evangeline found her voice first.

"You turned out tall. I always thought you would. You had long arm bones for a little girl. I wanted you to be tall. Strong."

"Well, I am." Jane laughed nervously.

"How did you get here?" Polite conversation to cover twelve silent years.

"I drove. The old jeep, remember it?" Jane told her about the flat tire, holding out the part of her blouse that had collected a black streak. The pointless story served as a softening so that at the end of it Jane could say, "I wish I'd come sooner. All these years."

"They don't allow visitors under eighteen anyhow, so you couldn't have come if you'd wanted to. And I'm glad you didn't. This isn't the way I wanted you to think of your mother."

"I know, but it's all right," Jane murmured, not knowing exactly what she meant by that.

But Evangeline nodded as though she knew. "Tell me about your rabbit business. Are you really making a living at it? Is it a good life for you?"

Jane's first genuine smile broke through the stiffness and illuminated her face. "I love it. At first I just started doing it . . . I don't know . . . I guess because the cages were there and I felt like I had to get away from Rogers or go

100

crazy. And since the place was mine—" Jane stumbled, "and because it was way out at the back of beyond, as my neighbor says, and I really needed to get away from people for a while, well, it just seemed like something I wanted to try. I didn't know if I'd be able to make any kind of living at all out of it, and of course there's not very much money in it, even with the fancy show stock. But it's a really good life. I'm beginning to feel like I accidentally made the perfect choice of how I wanted to live." Her happiness glowed in her face.

Evangeline looked subdued. "Was it terrible for you at Marlyce and Doyle's all those years? Were people cruel to you because of me?"

There was such deep apprehension in the question that Jane could not answer it honestly. "No, not really, just in my imagination mostly. Nobody threw rocks at me or anything." She tried to make a joke of it, but it was too near the nerve endings.

"Doyle and Marlyce? Did they—were they all right to you? I haven't had any contact with them in years."

"They were fine." Jane spoke carefully. Behind her eyes flashed pictures: Doyle weeping at the kitchen table for his dead brother, turning reddened eyes toward the small Janey as though she herself had pulled the trigger; Doyle speaking over Janey's head, telling neighbors about the tragic death of his brother in words that no child should have heard, surely not in connection with her own mother; Doyle giving birthday and Christmas presents to Marlyce but never to Janey. "She's not ours," he would say, looking his cold hate into her eyes.

"They were fine," she said again more firmly.

Evangeline looked steadily into Jane's face, and the look said she knew better. "I'm so sorry," she whispered.

Jane shook her head. "They didn't hurt me. You know that old saying, 'Whatever doesn't kill me makes me strong'? Well, I think Marlyce and Doyle sort of did that for me. I don't know how to explain it, but..."

Evangeline's hand covered Jane's and squeezed. "I know, daughter. These years have changed me, too, and not all for the worse. I have to ask you one thing, though, and I hope you tell me honestly because it's the most important thing in the world to me, and if you and I are going to have anything left out of this, we have to be honest about this one thing."

Jane nodded.

"I want you to tell me how you feel about . . . what I did."

"Shooting him."

"Yes. That."

"You had to do it," Jane said simply.

Evangeline rocked back and stared, trying to read the nuances of expression in Jane's face. "You know that?"

Again Jane nodded. "I always knew it. I used to try to tell that to Doyle and Marlyce but..." She shook her head. Better not to mention the three days locked in her bedroom closet after she'd tried to tell Doyle what her pa had been like.

"No," Evangeline agreed. "Doyle would never believe anything I tried to tell them about Ed, all the time we were married. Marlyce probably would have listened if it had been just her, but she couldn't stand up to Doyle. He and Ed were closer than most brothers, see. They didn't have any other family but just each other, and they'd always done everything together. Doyle and Marlyce cut their honeymoon trip short because those two brothers couldn't stand to be separated for more than a day or two. Ed and I never even tried to go anywhere.

"After we got married and moved out to Prosper, it seemed like Doyle and Marlyce were down every weekend without fail. The two of them men would go off fishing or setting trap lines or hunting squirrel or whatever, and Marlyce and I would sit and look at each other."

"Didn't either of you ever object?"

Evangeline shrugged. "Wouldn't have done any good. They were our husbands. What choice did we have?"

"Why did you marry him?" The question came out before Jane could censor it.

Her mother smiled a distant smile and shrugged. "I was thirty-one years old, and he was the only man that ever asked me."

"Were you terribly lonely, was that it?"

Again a shrug. "I don't know. Looking back, I don't think I was really truly lonely before I got married. It was just the idea of going through my whole life alone, never being chosen by any man. That bothered me a lot. It was such a public failure for a woman back then. Especially in a place like Prosper. Nobody ever thought a woman would stay single by choice. Oh, no. If you didn't get married it was because you weren't pretty enough. That was it. I expect I married just to prove I could."

They sat quietly, avoiding eye contact but thinking similar thoughts. Finally Jane said, "Couldn't you tell, before you married him..."

"That he was a secret wife-beater?" She smiled sadly and shook her head. "I knew he had a temper, but I had no idea he'd ever use it on me, much less on a little baby. On his own baby. It just seemed like once we were married, all the controls were off. He still thought like his daddy and granddaddy and all the men behind him. A wife was an absolute possession, and it was nobody's business how he treated her, not even the law's."

"Why didn't you report him to the police then, or to somebody?"

Evangeline sighed and stared at her memories. "He'd have killed me," she said simply. "He tried, twice, when he found out that I'd talked to Marlyce about it. Once the gun misfired and the other time he came after me with a skinning knife, but luckily he was drunk and I got it away from him and talked him down out of his mood."

"But why?" Jane anguished. "If he hated you that much, why didn't he leave you, or let you leave him?"

The woman shrugged. "The property was in my name, for one thing. At least it was at first. And you and I were his possessions, for another. I think he needed us. I think he was one of those men who hate women so much that they have to keep women around them just to torture. Ed's and Doyle's mother was a terrible woman. I think both of those boys got off to a warped start in life."

Jane thought, then said, "But if you'd turned him into the police for attempted murder those two times, wouldn't

104

he have gone to jail? We'd have been safe then, wouldn't we?"

"He might or might not have gone to jail. Most likely not. It would have been just my word against his. Doyle and Marlyce would never have testified against him, and he was always careful not to blow up at me in front of anyone else. Nor mark up my face when he beat on me. And you were too little to testify.

"If he'd actually killed me he'd probably have had to serve some time, but he'd have gotten out eventually, and he'd have come after you."

The enormity of her mother's sacrifice for her child came over Jane in a tide of realization.

They were silent for a long time. Finally Jane said, "When you turned yourself in, after you shot him, didn't you tell the police why you did it? Wouldn't they let you off on self-defense?"

Evangeline looked down. "I didn't want to get off. I killed him, and I knew I had to pay for it. I would have paid, in jail or out, but it seemed right to go to jail, to be out of your life while you were growing up. I tried to kill myself that day, but then I thought, who would drive you up to Rogers? And I couldn't let you see a sight like that. You were my baby."

Radio music and other voices filled the space between them. At length Jane said, "When will you be getting out?"

"I'm eligible for parole in ten months. I should have no trouble getting it. I'm not a threat to society." Her mouth twisted in a near-smile.

Jane nodded. "What will you do then?"

"Live. Get a job and just live. I'm using a computer in my job here in the library, and there are big companies around the state that hire women from here. I'll manage."

"You could come and live with me," Jane said, surprised at how strongly she meant it.

Evangeline shook her head. "I could never live in that house again, nor in Prosper. But..." Hesitantly she looked at Jane. "Maybe someplace not too far, where we could visit back and forth? Fayetteville or Fort Smith?"

Jane grinned a long, glowing grin and nodded. When she stood to go, they moved naturally into each other's arms for a hug so intense it squeezed moisture from their eyes.

ELEVEN

In October the air cooled and clarified, so that even in midafternoon Jane felt eager and full of energy. With the help of the jeep, the cleared road, and the now-familiar chain saw, by the middle of October she had amassed a woodpile, cut and stacked beside the house, that would last comfortably through the winter. With every load she brought out of the woods in the back of the jeep, she told herself she was buying a luxurious winter afternoon with a book.

She made the fall property tax payment with enough money left over, more than $900, to see her through the winter when the garden could no longer feed her completely, as it had done all summer.

Even with the cost of more and more rabbit feed and the monthly ad she now ran in the *Arkansas Rabbit Review,* the rabbitry was showing a profit. The *Review* ad and the roadside sign were bringing her buyers for her pedigreed New

Zealand bucks among other local breeders. And now, from time to time, the mail brought inquiries about show animals from the French Lops and the new Angora pairs that were beginning to produce.

In early November she took five of her best young Angoras and Lops to Harrison for the Northwest Arkansas Branch ARBA fall show, and came home with a second-place ribbon, two thirds, and a fourth, a good showing indeed for her first time out, the other exhibitors assured her. She raised her price five dollars for her show stock and took firm orders for four pair as soon as she had them to spare. She drove home grinning.

A few days later the fine weather broke. Chilly rain blew down from low, pewter skies, and Urchin refused to leave the house. Jane dug her winter jacket out of the box in the attic and zipped it up to her chin for the run to the barn. She did the chores in semidarkness, walking the rows of cages with her feed bucket under one arm, scooping pellets from bucket to feeders. She made notes of the three feeders that were still partly full from yesterday, so that by tomorrow she'd know whether they denoted a temporary lack of appetite or sickness that required treatment.

She ran to the spring for water, filled the empty water dishes, cleaned the catching trays of the night's collection of droppings and urine. The gray droppings lay on the dirt floor beneath the bottom row of cages, surprisingly odor-free, rotting into salable manure for next spring's gardeners, and covering a lively metropolis of fishworms to sell to Iva next year, for resale as fishbait.

Next, notebook in hand, she checked each of the does'

cages, peering into nest boxes to count the pink naked new-borns and to be sure there were no dead ones to be removed from box and list. A new litter of Lops had been kindled in the night, seven strong, uniformly sized babies. Four hundred twenty dollars' worth. She smiled.

One of the young Angoras had also kindled in the night, but there were only three babies. Jane shrugged philosophically and gave the doe her special new-litter treat, one lettuce leaf.

Back in the house, she fixed breakfast and ate it while reading a chapter in a Dick Francis mystery. The house felt deliciously cozy with both stove and fireplace ablaze and the rain blowing against the windows. Breakfast and chapter finished, she looked around for a job for the day and stared thoughtfully at the package of newly tanned hides that had come in the mail yesterday from the tanner. She thought about the display of rabbit-skin garments she'd seen at the ARBA show and especially about a plushy white fur vest she'd fingered, thinking, *I could make one of these.*

"Today's the day," she told herself. Hardly realizing she was singing, she opened the package and went to work, laying out pelts. Four of the pelts were from full-grown animals. The pelts were large enough that she only needed four, two for the front of the vest and two for the back.

Singing, "Fools rush in where wise men never go," she picked up the first pelt and began trimming it with her scissors, making straight lines out of animal-body contours. The leather was soft and pliable and velvety to the touch, lovely stuff to work with.

With a fresh cup of tea at her elbow and Urchin beside her

in the chair, complaining softly about the squeeze between hip and chair, Jane began to join two pelts, making careful whipstitches with tough carpet thread she'd bought to repair the raveling rag rug in the bedroom.

She began to wonder how much of her wardrobe might be made from rabbit skins. Grinning, she pictured white-fur underwear and jeans.

By lunchtime, three of the four long seams were finished, leaving only the last side seam and some sort of hemming around neck, armholes, and bottom edge. She laid it aside with stiff fingers and made lunch, leftovers of last night's catfish with stewed tomatoes and green peppers, and chunks of zucchini under melted cheese. All free, she mused with satisfaction, all except the cheese, and that she'd got from Iva in a fryer trade.

After she'd eaten, she dipped hot water from the stove's reservoir and washed the dishes in the dishpan in the plumbingless sink. As she worked she figured again the cost of piping water down from the spring and putting in real plumbing. It would cost too much for now, she knew, as would the electrical wiring and refrigerator and freezer that would ease her daily chores.

But those things were coming. She knew it. Gradually, next year or the year after or whenever there was enough money, those things would come, as this year the rabbit stock and the jeep and chain saw had come, giving her her start. *All in good time,* she told herself. *And meanwhile I'm okay as I am.*

She had just settled into her sewing again when she was startled by a knock at the door. She looked up with a welcoming smile, expecting Iva or Marian.

110

But the face peering in through the glass belonged to Marlyce. Jane let her in. "What are you doing clear out here?" Her voice was carefully curious, neither welcoming nor cold.

Marlyce stepped in and shed her plastic raincoat. "Can I come in?"

"Sure." Jane stood aside while Marlyce looked slowly around. With a vague movement of her hand she invited her guest to sit at the table.

"Don't tell me you just happened to be in the neighborhood."

"I came down to see you, to see how you were getting along." Marlyce's eyes seemed to be asking for something. Pardon?

"After eleven months?" Jane sounded more bitter than she'd intended.

"I couldn't . . . Doyle wouldn't let me . . . I took a day off from work to come down here, Jane. If he finds out, he'll kill me, but I wanted to be sure you were all right. Are you?"

"I'm fine, thank you." Jane motioned around her.

"Are you really?" Marlyce seemed unsure. "I didn't know if you'd still be here even. I figured you might have moved off someplace and got a job. What are you doing?"

"Raising rabbits, like I said I was going to."

"And you can live on that?"

Jane nodded. She picked up the fur vest and began sewing a small hem around one arm hole. Let Marlyce talk, she thought, she's the one who came here.

But Marlyce sat wordlessly, looking around the shabby kitchen, thinking her own thoughts.

"Cup of tea?" Jane said finally, feeling uncomfortably inhospitable.

"No, thanks. I was just thinking, I spent a lot of hours in this room back in the old days."

"With my mother."

"Yeah."

"I went to see her last month."

Marlyce looked startled. "You went to see Evangeline? In prison? Uh, how is she?"

"Very well, thank you. We got acquainted a little bit. I liked her. When she gets out next year, she's going to get a job in Fayetteville so we can be close to each other."

There was a note of vengeance in her voice that surprised even Jane. She said, "How come you never went to see her all those years, or let me write to her? I should have been writing to her."

Hesitantly Marlyce said, "Janey, you never had a chance to, well, understand how things were with the four of us, Vangie and me, Doyle and Eddie."

"How could I understand if nobody ever told me?"

"I know. Well, you were too young, and it seemed like the best thing to do was just not to bring up any of that, that happened. Best let you forget about it as much as you could."

"Okay, so I'm older now," Jane said woodenly. "So tell me."

Marlyce shrugged and gouged into the wooden tabletop with her thumbnail. "See, those boys were awful close, Doyle and Eddie. Their mama was an old tartar, always telling those two little boys that men were cruel, filthy beasts, making them hate themselves really. They grew up hating their mama for making them feel like scum of the earth, and I think it made them turn against women in general. It also made them hang on to each other more than most brothers, out of sheer self-defense."

"What was their father like?" Jane asked, her curiosity rising.

"Basically not worth a dead cat's whisker. Every once in a while he'd go on a toot and get plastered and beat up on his wife, knock the boys around some to prove his manhood, and then he'd go back to being just kind of a shadow in the background. I barely remember what he looked like. He was no match for Mama Cahill, that's for sure."

They followed their own thoughts silently for a minute. Then Marlyce said, "Doyle was always the stronger one of them two boys. He led and Eddie followed. Just between you and me, I think the only reason Eddie married Vangie was because Doyle married me, and I had one hell of a job getting him to the altar. It seemed like Eddie was his first priority always. Never me."

Pain and resentment showed through her words, making Jane ponder for the first time Marlyce's feelings.

"Well, at first it seemed like maybe things were going to work out okay after we all got married. I mean, Vangie and I were best friends. She was working in Rogers trying to earn money to go to college on. That was her big dream. She was crazy about books, and her big dream was to work in a library, so she'd been working up in Rogers, trying to save up tuition money. These people that were some relation of hers had this cafe there, and she and I were both waitressing there that one summer. I don't think you ever knew them. They sold out and moved to Colorado before you were born, so you wouldn't have. I was engaged to

113

Doyle, so naturally Vangie started going with Eddie, since he came along on most of our dates anyway."

Jane thought about her mother having fierce dreams and working so hard to make them come true and then achieving them finally in so bizarre a way.

"So then what happened?"

"Well, then when you were born, that's when things started falling apart."

Jane tilted her head like a bird listening for the underground worm. Doyle's bastard? Was it true, then?

"See," Marlyce said, looking down, "Doyle and me couldn't have children. He had mumps when he was in the service, and it left him sterile."

Jane thought, *That answers that.*

"He never told anyone. He didn't even tell Eddie, he was so ashamed. I kept telling him it didn't bother me, I never really wanted kids anyhow, but that just made him madder. So then when Vangie and Eddie had you, it seemed like it just killed something between those two brothers. Doyle pulled away, like. He'd say little cutting things to Eddie, trying to belittle him, and I know it drove Eddie nuts. He didn't understand what was going on. I remember him saying once that he wished you'd never been born. I know it didn't have anything to do with you personally, it was just that he couldn't stand Doyle cutting him off like that. Neither one of those guys ever loved anybody but each other."

Slow understanding seeped through Jane. A tangle of love and vindictiveness and neurotic needs, ending with an explosion in a bedroom, in a house in a clearing. And the reverberations went on in the lives of everyone involved.

TWELVE

Before she left that day, Marlyce stood at the door looking up at Jane, studying her. "You've changed a lot since you've been out here, you know that?"

"Changed how?" The stiffness was gone from Jane's voice by now.

Marlyce pondered, frowned, said, "I don't know. You've aged."

Jane grinned and gave the woman a sudden, swooping hug. "I'm glad you came."

"Yeah. Me, too. Are you sure you won't come for Christmas? Doyle won't say anything, I promise."

Jane shook her head. "I appreciate the invitation, I really do. But I can't leave the rabbits that long. And I've got plans for Christmas here, with friends. But it means a lot to me that you invited me."

The next day Jane butchered and dressed out sixteen adult does, the last of the Shaffley animals. It would cut drastically into her Freez-Fine checks for a few months, but the sixteen inferior does would be replaced by January with good young pedigreed does, making her entire herd high quality. Then, she reasoned, she'd be able to sell at least half of her young to other breeders, raising her profit considerably.

The sixteen roaster-sized carcasses went into a newly rented locker at the locker plant in Prosper. It was a white, concrete-block building just off Main Street, where people with insufficient freezer space could rent cold storage for a quarter of beef or a side of pork, or just for an overflow of garden produce. Jane traded a few of the roasters to the Smiths for bacon and chops, since they had recently bought a side of pork in conjunction with another couple from their church.

The sixteen large hides went off to the tanner with a rush request and were back within a week, stiff oily rabbit skin turned into supple, velvety suede.

The first snow came, a light whipped-cream covering of emerald grass and still-bright oak leaves. Urchin walked on tiptoe, distastefully shaking the white stuff off each paw as she lifted it. Jane closed the big barn doors for the winter and began covering the jeep with an old tarp to keep the seat dry. She lined the does' nest boxes with squares of cardboard for insulation and worried about water dishes freezing and breaking.

After the sun-gilded snow came days of dismal, freezing rain, sometimes mixed with sleet or snow or both. Except for the necessary barn chores and the daily trips to the spring for water and dashes to the outhouse, postponed as long as possible, Jane stayed in the house.

She spent most of her time working with the sixteen hides, trimming them and stitching them together with a glow that was part anticipation, part simple pleasure at her creations.

On an afternoon when it wasn't actually raining or snowing, she unwrapped the jeep and drove to Fayetteville with a load of pet-shop bunnies, Lops and Angoras not quite good enough to sell to show fanciers. In the mall she used some of the bunny money to buy pieces of sweater-knit material and matching heavyweight thread—red, green, blue, and black. Then, deciding this would be her Christmas present to herself, she bought three yards of dark-green velvet.

Then, having spent so much money already that the bars of caution were down, she went into the Wal-Mart and bought Christmas-tree decorations. As she picked them out she was conscious of beginning her own personal Christmas traditions. These decorations, she knew, would be part of her Christmases maybe for the rest of her life, Christmases to be shared with her mother, her friends—possibly a husband, possibly not, but the traditions would be hers, no matter what.

Back home, she worked intensely, experimenting, holding her breath as she cut into the expensive knit material, breathing out in a whoosh of relief when corners and edges came together as they should. Sometimes she laughed out loud at the goodness of life, and at Urchin curled on the pile of material scraps with a strand of red knit over one eye.

By the end of the week her creations were finished. For her mother there was a beautiful rabbit-fur pullover sweater, the body made of four hides, as Jane's original vest had been, but with the addition of blue knit sleeves, turtleneck, and waist cuff. The effect was that of a fur vest worn over a blue sweater, strikingly attractive and plushy warm.

For Marian, the same thing, with black trim to go with her black hair, and for Marlyce, the original vest with red knit additions. Beau and Iva had presented more of a problem because four hides weren't enough to go around them. Beau's sweater, then, had black sleeves and collar and also black knit insets down the sides and down the front, which Jane finished off with buttons, cardigan style. Iva's was similar, with green trim.

She realized that omitting Doyle from her list was obvious and probably unkind, but the memory of all of those Christmases and birthdays in his house with no presents for Janey, that was too big a hurdle for her to get past. *Maybe next year,* she thought. *Or maybe not.*

The weather warmed and brightened the next day. With her chain saw and the jeep she drove up the timber road and brought home a small spruce tree. There had been a bigger one, fat and full and glorious but simply too big for her present space. "In a few years," she told the tree, "when I can afford to build on to the house, then watch out, buster. I'm coming back for you."

Plans were spinning in her head: a slant-roofed addition across the back of the house with bathroom and bedroom. Then her present bedroom could be a genuine living room with comfortable chairs for visitors, so her friends wouldn't have to sit around the kitchen table. The fireplace would

118

have bookshelves around it, and there would be electricity, a comfortable reading light behind the sofa, for winter afternoons with her books, and a little television set for evenings.

Not everything all at once, she reminded herself, but gradually, as she could afford it. A genuine twentieth-century life like everyone else's, but all her own, earned by her own wit and work.

Ideas were blossoming almost faster than she could pluck and examine them. With her Christmas sewing done and nothing pressing to do beyond daily chores, she spent those afternoons before Christmas sketching and figuring in a new spiral notebook that she kept beside her bed now. Designs grew from idea to idea. The vest she'd started for herself had suggested the gift sweater vests; they suggested rabbit fur slippers for children, cute little warm slippers furry inside and out, with soles reinforced with tough vinyl she'd seen in the fabric store.

And mittens. Matching sets of caps and mittens for children. Maybe stuffed toy rabbits in a comical floppy pose.

Most of all she loved the figuring: Sweater vests cost about four dollars to make, for the knit material, maybe cheaper if she watched sale tables and discount stores; half a day's work once she got into the swing of it; two dollars for tanning the hides; say an average cost of seven-fifty including thread, and buttons for the cardigan styles. Sell them for forty dollars apiece to boutiques and specialty shops, who could retail them for seventy.

Or sell them herself for seventy at craft fairs.

The small items, slippers and mittens, could be made from

hides of young fryer-sized rabbits, she thought, *if only I were government-inspected so I could sell the meat directly to the public instead of through Freez-Fine.*

Well, why not? I could at least find out what kind of facilities and equipment I'd need to pass the inspection. If I could legally sell my meat, I bet I could sell everything I wanted just locally, all the ones I couldn't sell as breeders or show animals. Five dollars a rabbit, like I've been trading to Iva for. Everybody's so health- and weight-conscious now, and rabbit meat is lower in calories and fat and higher in protein than any other meat, and it's delicious. With a little advertising...and then I'd have all those hides to make slippers and mittens out of.

"And the Angoras," she said to Urchin. "Wow, what would people pay for those gorgeous shaggy woolly hides in slippers and sweater-vests? It's all there waiting for me, Urch, all it takes is work. And cleverness. *Damn*, I'm good!"

She laughed aloud.

The Smiths were going to their son's for Christmas, so Jane invited them for dinner two nights before, along with Iva. She baked a ham and decorated the two rooms with branches cut from evergreens in the woods. When the dirty work was done, she dressed in the lace blouse and the new green velvet skirt, which swept elegantly to the floor. Her hair caught glints of firelight in its waves and set off a face that was beautiful in its strength and joy and sheer character.

She admired herself in the mirror and thought, *Aaron Bruns can just eat his heart out. He doesn't realize what a great woman he passed up.* There was no pain left in the thought of Aaron.

The house glowed with readiness. The ham perfumed the air, along with the spruce tree in the kitchen corner, awaiting its decorations. That would be done later, with friends to share the ceremony.

"This will be one of my Christmas traditions," she decided. "I'll always have a party and invite everyone I like, and we'll decorate the tree together. That way I won't start feeling lonely and sorry for myself. There are all kinds of love, after all. Urchin, get down out of that tree. That is not a cat-climbing tree, and if you break any of my new decorations when they get hung, I'm going to be peddling catskin mittens. Do you get the message?"

Urchin settled herself more comfortably across the branches next to the tree's trunk and dug her claws luxuriously into the bark.

When it grew dark and nearly time, Jane went to the door and stood where she could watch for the first gleam of headlights through the trees. Although Marlyce had been unable to identify it, there was a quality about Jane that had grown in this year, from invisibly present to strongly apparent.

It had grown from the courage of that first decision, to come to this place and carve a life from it. It had fed on past pain. "All that doesn't kill me makes me strong." It expanded with the conquering of the first killed doe, the first solo trip into the woods with the potentially dangerous chain saw.

It blossomed fully open when Jane Cahill embraced her mother, and her aunt. Now it shone from a face made handsome by accomplishment.

It was dignity.